To Honor the Dead

Joseph W. Shaw

UNIVERSITY OF NEW MEXICO PRESS   ALBUQUERQUE

13 12 11 10 09 08   1 2 3 4 5 6

Library of Congress Cataloging-in-Publication Data

Shaw, Joseph W., 1944–
  To honor the dead / Joseph W. Shaw.
     p. cm.
ISBN 978-0-8263-3999-7 (cloth : alk. paper)
1. Truck drivers—Fiction. 2. Oklahoma—Fiction. 3. Psychological fiction. I. Title.
 PS3619.H3934T6 2008
 813'.6—dc22

                         2007031861

Book design and type composition by Melissa Tandysh
Composed in 10.5/14.5 Palatino LT Std ❧ Display type is Bodoni Std
Printed on 50# Natures Natural

Dedication

To those old Indians (they would have scoffed at the more politically correct "senior Native Americans,") whom I remember from my childhood:

To Sam Rivers, who wore bits of thin red yarn woven into his iron gray braids when he came to town on Saturday; and Myrtle Lincoln, who presented my wife and me with a little blue velvet frock on the occasion of the birth of our first daughter; and to Katie Osage, that ancient, frail repository of tribal wisdom, of whom my mother thought so much; to Old Man Gold, good friend of my grandfather, and cavalry scout out of Ft. Reno in the very last days of hostilities, whose death a few years before my time nevertheless left in me a sense of connection to the history of my part of the world; to Jim Whiteplume, kind and gentle soul who, knowing my interest in such things, once gave me a treasured relic of pipestone, and in whose creaking old wagon with the matched team of mules I rode away the hours and days of my early summers; and, of course, to Mary Mixed Hair, who I'm told changed my diapers, and whose warm smile and capable hands cared for my grandmother through the early part of her dying.

There were others, too—lined faces of old leather, a friendly nod, watching with bemused indifference the frantic comings and goings of commerce in our little prairie town. I'm ashamed to say I never knew their names.

I honor their memory.

Acknowledgments

First and foremost I want to thank my wife, Gina, my best friend and partner in business and in life for forty-three years, without whose loving support and undying confidence I would never have finished this daunting task.

I also wish to thank, in order of their appearance, those special mentors, my writing coaches and teachers: Louis (Johnny) Johnson, Tony Hillerman, Lois Duncan, Gordon Weaver, and Paula Paul. A special thanks to Tony, his lovely wife, Marie, and to Paula, for their thoughtful reading of the manuscript, their helpful suggestions, and their kind and enthusiastic encouragement. A special thanks, also, to Morris Eaves of the University of New Mexico's English Department, whose long-ago guidance through an exhaustive, intense, and passionate explication of Faulkner's *The Sound and the Fury* over the course of a semester left me, leaves me still, in breathless awe of such literary talent. We learn to write by reading, and Professor Eaves taught me to read.

When the student is ready, the teacher appears. I could not have become who I am, let alone written anything of value, without all of you.

Thanks, also, to my good friend David Schneider, who first brought the manuscript to the attention of Luther Wilson, director of UNM Press. Thanks too, Luther, for listening!

By the way, I should mention that this is a book of fiction. Nothing in it is true. I made it all up, and if anything in it even remotely resembles a grain of truth, it's purely coincidental. I honestly tried to keep to the lie. I owe to my mentors the degree to which I am successful in making you believe the lie. The degree to which I fail remains a failure all my own.

And finally, a cautionary note on the characters' language: it's bad.

At times, very bad. My late aunt, Nadeen Willis, said people shouldn't talk that way, but what can I do. The characters insist on saying those things.

If you are one who is bothered by bad language, I have a suggestion: when you come to a bad word, don't read it. Just skip over it and go on to the next one. That way you won't be offended, and the larger meaning can easily be gathered from context. In those rare instances where the second and third words are as bad as the first, however, you're on your own.

Once, there was a poor orphan. . . .
—Plains Indian tale

Prologue

✥ Blaine County, Oklahoma, September 1956

On an unseasonably warm Saturday morning in September, the month of sunflowers, two Indian boys, half brothers dressed alike in faded blue Levi's, T-shirts, and new Keds black-top sneakers, walk quietly along the railroad tracks in the heat, two isolate points advancing upon a long, slow arc. The boys proceed in single file, the way everyone knows Indians walk, each boy balancing one foot carefully in front of the other on the polished steel rail while they occasionally argue over who will carry a small rifle brought along for rabbits.

The little rifle, a war souvenir their uncle packed home from Korea, consists of a short, milled stainless steel tube for a barrel, which holds a single .22 long-rifle round in the chamber, and a simple three-piece, spring-loaded trigger and firing pin assembly on a molded stock of heavy-gauge aluminum rod. Designed as a fighter pilot's survival rifle, the little gun looks more like a toy than anything else. It is very lightweight and fun to shoot, and even though the gun belongs to his older brother Johnny, Oliver is determined to carry it his share of the time.

"Come on, Johnny," he complains. "My goddamn turn."

Johnny, who is three years older and, even though the shorter of the two, has always been able to do everything faster and better and is therefore still in charge, is fastwalking away along the rail with the rifle.

"Fuck you, Ollie," he says over his shoulder. "I told you, not till we get to the cellar."

"Shithead."

The boys' destination, their secret hideout when they were little and could still play freely with the owner's grandson, a white boy named Cole Tyree, lies far away across the broad valley, hidden from view in a green grove of chinaberry trees at the lower end of a neglected pasture long since gone back to thistle and cedar and sandhill plum. The boys know the plum thicket on the old Tyree place to be a sure haven for rabbits, but they also know there are graves hidden in the low dunes, burials so old only their grandparents' grandparents might have known the people buried there. The boys know of the graves from the tiny bright red and blue beads and bleached white bits of bone scattered among the bare, wind-eroded roots of the dwarf plums. Because of the burials, the sandy plum thicket was a sacred and haunted place when they were much younger, and out of respect they still will not kill anything there. But beyond the plum thicket and across the marshy little spring-fed creek choked with cattails, an old, fenced-in root cellar and springhouse, dug deep into the hillside at the edge of the chinaberry grove, barely shows its dome of red brick and mortar above the earth. Old, old hunting magic lingers in the dappled sunlight and silence of the chinaberry grove, and anything that moves is fair game.

The railroad tracks shimmer away into the distance, while underfoot the steel rail pops every so often with minute expansions in the rising heat. The boys' T-shirts are damp from sweat so that even the lightest breeze feels cool as it rustles and stirs among the sunflowers. Obsessed with his mission to kill a rabbit with the little rifle, Oliver prods his brother on toward the cellar. On the way the older boy proves himself with a pinging sound off a green glass insulator high on the crossbar of a telephone pole, but even Johnny is not a good enough shot to down their first rabbit. Bounding away into the dense cover of Johnson grass and sunflowers along the right-of-way fence, the fleeing rabbit makes Oliver's heart seem to skip a beat.

As the tracks climb slowly out of the valley and onto the ridge above the chinaberry grove and its secret, vaulted cellar, Johnny stalks ahead more carefully, keeping the gun at the ready. Oliver, more than a little irritated now with the heat and the distance and the monotony of sunflowers, trails impatiently along behind like Coyote, rehearsing a precision dash and grab. He jumps with abandon from crosstie to crosstie, then feints into a silent, balanced rush, one foot in front of the other along the smooth steel rail, anticipating from some such clever ambush the spoils of victory and a perfectly counted coup.

❧ Easter Sunday, April 3, 1994

Chapter One

Nearly forty years later, on Easter morning, April 3, 1994, sunrise breaks with a flood of orange light across the east ridge of an old homestead quarter of brushy creek bottom and hillside winter wheat, the light flaring onto the scratched outer lens of a pair of worn field glasses.

The farm, with its long-abandoned outbuildings and corrals, lies two miles north and a mile east of the town of Fairview, in extreme western Blaine County, Oklahoma. From just inside the partially open door of a nearly collapsed barn, a tall and grotesquely obese white man sitting on two side-by-side folding chairs commands a narrow view to the east along the creek. At the very moment sunlight clears the ridge, the man winces at the explosion of light in the glasses. This far from town he can only just hear the monotonous tolling of the steeple bell from the First Baptist Church announcing sunrise services.

Save for the one set of footprints and the dog's meandering trail that he can see with the glasses, the snow along the creek lies blue and undisturbed, deep in early morning shadow. The man can see clearly Tyree's sleeper cab parked up near the railroad tracks on the far hill across the valley. Through the still morning air he can hear, over the tolling of the bell, the distant, irregular coughing of the diesel engine, set at slow idle to keep the fuel in the tanks from jelling overnight in the iron cold. The man retreats out of sight beneath the fallen roof, careful to stay beyond the sudden reach of sunlight on the cold, manured floor, and watches for any further sign of movement.

All in all a pretty farm, the man thinks, looking out over winterbare trees that trace a bend in the creek. He likes the way the stiff tangle of Johnson grass and cattail hangs bent above the snowdrifts, and how the ragged bottomland along the creek gives way to the hardedged fields of bright green winter wheat climbing in thin, terraced rows up both sides of the valley. He thinks it must have been quite a place when the older Tyrees occupied the two-story farmhouse now burned to blackened ruin just uphill of the barn. He wonders if they had even known about the graves dug into the sand hills high along the east end of the place next to the tracks. The one intact skull he's found over there is a real windfall. He knows that the skull, along with burial offerings of stone pipes and cheap Mexican silver conchos, the few beads of elk tooth and cowry shell, and a handful of flint arrowpoints he's dug up for mail order shipment couldn't date back much beyond the mid-1800s. Before that he knows the Cheyenne were still leaving their dead up on willow scaffolds for the owls and crows to get at. And he wonders, too, why it took the only Tyree heir so long to come home and lay claim to the place, ruining everything.

Well, the man thinks, timing is everything.

Cradling a Marlin .30–30 lever-action rifle like some child's plaything on his huge lap, he once again leans closer to the doorway and takes up the glasses, alert for the quick movements of a coyote. Too bad the gig had to go sour. Sooner or later, though, they all went sour. It was a pattern he didn't care to examine too closely. Life was surely a mystery, all right. With his view interrupted only by a scattering of cedars along the creek, the man can see clearly that he and Tyree are alone, and despite his agenda, the spread of the empty valley makes him feel strangely at peace.

Less than half a mile away Oliver Lonewolf stands motionless, invisible even, behind a tall stand of winter-dry Johnson grass next to the creek. He studies the double trail of shadowed footprints where his old friend, Cole Tyree, and the dog have struggled through deep snow-drifts at the base of a low hill. Except for his two brief overseas tours in the Nam, the first one cut short by a little miniclaymore wired to a bicycle left beside the trail, the second when the whole fucking army turned and ran, Oliver Lonewolf has watched over the farm for close to forty years now.

Oliver began his vigil long before Cole Tyree grew up and moved away, and in all that time, no one, not even that fat, arrogant, squaw-bashing, wolf-killing, grave-robbing motherfucker hiding in the barn has ever posed a threat.

∼ **Friday, April 1, 1994**

Chapter Two

Two days earlier, at around three in the morning along a wintry stretch of Interstate 40 just east of the Oklahoma-Texas line, fifty-plus-year-old Colter Wayne Tyree dozed off at the wheel of his reefer van, a twenty-four-thousand-pound tractor-trailer rig running dry and empty at nearly seventy miles an hour.

Dreaming a much younger version of himself walking arm in arm across the tarmac with a graveyard shift waitress from the Petro Truck Palace outside Amarillo, Colter had just spotted a skinhead scrawling "Satan Lives!" on the mud-spattered driver's door of his old White cab-over tractor. He was about to draw down with his nickel-plated, snub-nosed little .32 semi and send the tattooed punker on home to Jesus when the truck ran smack over something and made him blink.

The sudden flash of tawny brown at the lower left edge of his head-light beam, a rapid series of dull thumps as the object tumbled and flopped beneath the forty-two feet of trailer, and a final, sickening bump at the right rear duals brought Colter bolt awake at the wheel. Adrenaline and pattern recognition kicked in all at once, and he knew instantly he had just run over a coyote. The reefer van, licensed out of Albuquerque, belonged to Roadrunner Freight, an irony not altogether wasted on Colter despite the panic of the moment. He steadied his grip on the wheel, feathering the brake pedal with his bare left foot, and shuddered, first for the poor, mangled animal, and then at the very real possibility of his own twelve-ton coffin hurtling through the dark, out of control at around one hundred feet per second on a thin, invisible skin of ice. Despite the bravado of his dreams, Colter was very much afraid to die. His smoldering anger at Marilyn, so carefully nurtured for the last three hundred miles, was gone in an instant. The coyote, flat as his cartoon cousin by now, had probably just saved Colter's life.

Colter had never been one for religious fervor, but he had long ago learned to recognize divine intervention when it hit him over the head. Problem was, it never lasted. With his glove-box stash down to less than a thousand dollars cash and a flashlight full of leaky Evereadys, just touching the warm Bakelite grip of the hefty little semiautomatic wedged in beside his seat gave Colter a moment of reassurance against the enormous dark beyond the light snow beginning to fall into his headlight beams.

Jesus, he thought again.

Catching himself, trying for his center again to let the adrenaline melt away, Cole Tyree could feel the accumulated weight of all five decades and forty-odd extra pounds pressing all the way down onto the soles of his bare feet. Thinking maybe he deserved a break from all this shit. Full retirement was obviously out of the question since he couldn't even say for sure where next month's truck payment was coming from. But maybe just a little time off to smell the roses. Awful tired lately, too. Maybe go in for a checkup, find out why the hell he can't pop a benny or two and drive all day and all night the way he could way back when he was only forty. Through it all, the old tan Labrador riding second seat hadn't even stirred.

Chapter Three

Thinking of the hapless coyote and of his own uncertain future, Colter smiled in the dark at Leon the Labrador, still sound asleep with his head vibrating on the console between the seats. Left over from Colter's crumbling marriage along with a boxed, incomplete set of green and white World Book Encyclopedias and not much else, the dog had traveled nearly a million miles with him. By now Leon had seen most of the good old USA from the elevated vantage point of the passenger-side window. Already eleven years old, with a graying muzzle and sad, bloodshot eyes, Leon had worn himself out with uneasiness for the first few thousand miles, sniffing constantly and looking out at the countryside. He had struggled mightily with his bladder and his new, loftier view of things, but in the end Colter knew the dog had simply learned to trust once again in his truest and best friend. He had fallen quietly asleep in the passenger seat and had awakened only rarely in the two years since.

Colter knew one of these days he was really going to miss that dog, pain in the ass or not. And when it happened he was afraid the fragile ties to his marriage, his old life, would finally break. Now, driving alone late into the night, lost in the private, anonymous void of the road with his eyes misting over for no good reason at all, he allowed himself a quiet moment of reflection on some of the doors that might be closing.

"And miles to go before I sleep," he whispered hopefully, remembering a little high school Frost, but Leon never stirred.

Flipping the heater up another click, Colter couldn't imagine allowing the rest of his allotted years to waste away like the last two had, slowly shrinking out of sight into his chrome side mirrors. Just the same, he sure as hell didn't want them disappearing all at once. The dash lights of the darkened cab hadn't even flickered as the coyote crossed over into coyote heaven. He slapped his face once to make sure he was actually awake and hadn't dreamed the coyote, too, and immediately felt the sweat on his right palm. His digital Timex blinked out 3:32 AM mountain standard, the dashboard gauges were all looking good, and Colter's world went right on spinning.

Occasionally Colter had the vague impression that it was only his tires that made the world turn; that the claustrophobic, rolling tomb he now called home actually floated, stationary, above an endless highway while his whining drive duals spun the earth beneath him. Day after night after day he watched the pavement suck down under the little plastic dashboard saint as if life were only an elaborate video game. You dodged the bumps or went "boom." Enough booms, game over.

Wide awake now, forebrain focused on glowing dashboard gauges and the look of the icy roadway ahead, Colter figured each additional mile was beginning to buck the odds. So many gone already. Go far enough back, there was one only he and the Devil knew about, and neither of them were talking just yet.

Colter had skipped right through the minefield of Vietnam as a stateside training officer, but he had lost two close buddies and a cousin to that war. Caught up in a morbid accounting, he could also name a couple of company drivers recently dead in a nasty truck pileup, and more than a few lifelong acquaintances fallen to cancer. Or like his father, for chrissake, whom Colter had come to see as some indestructible force of nature, dropped stone dead just last year of a sudden heart attack. When he thought about it, which he seemed to be doing a lot of since his father's death and his own last birthday, Colter had begun to sense an urgency, a quickening of the pace.

Taking runs he might have passed up six months ago, mostly for the money but partly to keep from having to think too much about the mess his life was in, Colter had deadheaded all the way to Amarillo just to grab the empty reefer van. Dispatch had booked him a load of swinging beef at Packingtown out by the Okie City stockyards with drive-away set no later than Saturday noon. He was dog-tired already, and it would mean fudging a little on the logbook, but God how he needed that load.

The "tentative" separation from Marilyn, intended as a rational and calm cooling off period, a time to find himself again after the failure of his freight distribution business in New Mexico, had backfired. His two daughters, long since flown from their dysfunctional nest to other places, now had their own lives, their own demons. All their separate paths rarely crossed. While Marilyn laid the groundwork for independence and a successful new career selling upscale real estate in Albuquerque, Cowboy Colter was still looking for himself, and by now the search was beginning to feel a little frantic.

Deciding what to do about Marilyn was not going to be easy, and he knew if he waited much longer the decision wouldn't be his to make anymore. That's where things got a little fuzzy.

He knew what lay on each side of the highway in the dark, Texas night. He could see, in his mind's eye, the rolling fields that stretched away to the horizon, the distant grain elevators almost but not quite out of sight beyond the gentle curve of the earth. He knew the shape and feel of the country that lay ahead, the way the patchwork quilting of the snowy fields would look from the air, the thin, cross-stitched lace of cottonwood and willow and stunted elm along the upland creeks of western Oklahoma. He had a sense of the landscape caught in the grip of this late spring storm. He could even imagine the white-washed, silent look of his old hometown, buried beneath its winter shroud an hour ahead just off the interstate, but for the life of him, Colter couldn't, with any certainty, imagine next week.

Since the failure of his business a couple years back, he had hidden in the tiny six-by-eight sleeper cab, his only remaining rig. Driving was how he had started, and it was something he could still do even when everything else went south. In the beginning the cab had been his home away from home. It was a refuge he left only rarely, for an occasional step down onto the glistening tarmac of a rain-slick truck stop parking lot for a meal, a pit stop, some idle waitress gab over a hot cup of coffee. The vast interstate highway system had seemed at the time like one long, exciting string of lights running coast to coast, border to border. He had lost himself in the movement of it, the company dream come true: a stable, dependable, independent driver who lived only for the next dispatch, the lure of the road.

Since the beginning he had felt tethered to Marilyn, home, his real life, by invisible elastic bands that stretched taut but never quite gave way. The return runs through Albuquerque were like the headlong rush of a fall; he could feel himself caught up in the relentless, accelerating pull of gravity. And then, after a day, a week, it would all fall apart again just in time to hit the highway. But now, after two years alone on the road, the darkened sleeper cab, once a symbol of the purest kind of freedom, Colter now found confining, frightening. Lately he could hardly choke back a claustrophobic vision of his own fate, upside down somewhere and buried alive inside that small, terrifying space while the world went on without him. Truth be known, he couldn't imagine how drivers for the Batesville Casket Company kept going at all. It was so bad that Colter had recently taken to driving with the window down, no small inconvenience just now, running blind into the southern sweep of a late-season Great Plains storm.

Rolling along wide awake and barefoot at a cautious thirty-five miles an hour through the dark panhandle night, his toes basking in the flow of warm air from the heater and his eyes now alert for the coming snowpack and treacherous black ice along I-40, Colter pursued his personal inventory in silent anxiety mode.

Day or night, vague feelings of depression and regret had often haunted him for the two-hour pull through that bleak, flat stretch of interstate outside Amarillo, but near Shamrock the country began to change again. Now, coming down off the barren High Plains country of the Texas panhandle, he could feel the hills rolling away in the dark, could sense the road begin to break away from its monotonous eastering. Colter could almost always feel his pulse quicken as he crossed the Oklahoma line. He felt like he had driven this stretch of interstate, east to west, west to east, and back again a thousand times or more. Often enough the schedule had been too tight to wiggle anyway, but if he was honest about it, he knew there were times he should have turned off at mile marker 132 and pushed the couple of miles north to home. But he hadn't. Couldn't. Not even for his father's recent funeral. Seemed to Colter at the time it was still one body over the limit to deal with. Couldn't bear the risk of shattering his illusions yet, either. He still needed the past intact. At least that. He just needed a little more time, that's all. Colter had been a grown-up for a long time now, but after all the ups and downs were tallied he still didn't amount to shit, and he hadn't set foot in his childhood home since before Jack Kennedy was shot.

Godalmighty, what those upstanding citizens must have thought years ago when the going got tough and he just up and left. In light of his family's prominence the citizens of Fairview certainly wouldn't have predicted the protruding paunch, the sweat-stained Stetson he wore to hide his receding hairline, the poverty and failure that had overtaken him like a lie one day at a time. Now, nearly forty years later, he didn't think he could bear the look in their eyes.

One of these days he knew he'd have to take that dreaded exit and then the little two-lane State Road 33 spur. With his father gone, he'd maybe deal with the farm, the only thing left in the estate now after his mother's slow, costly demise. See to a gravestone, maybe. Marilyn was right. The old man deserved at least that. Maybe even check on the remaining cemetery plot mentioned in the will. He knew for a fact there were worse places to end up than that little cedar-covered knoll overlooking the river south of town. Or drive out past the lake again. He had always pictured himself coming home some summer and turning into the Texaco station at the four-way stop pulling a brand-new, blue and white twenty-foot Bayliner. But not now. Not yet. Dreams die hard. Then, just east of Sayre, in the interstate's first wide curve away to the north, he noticed a rig pulled off on the narrow shoulder, the driver pulling his tire chains out of the side box.

Within minutes there were eleven more rigs off to the side, their running lights ablaze in a long, curving string, festive as Christmas along the interstate. He wished again he had fixed the CB. Some of the old chatter might help him stay awake, but until he picked up his voucher at the stockyards, he'd be satisfied, thank you very much, just not to have anything else break down. The little glove-box stash would see him through, and be damned if he would call Marilyn for money again.

Checking his dependable Timex against radio time, Colter gathered from fifty thousand watts of WNOE New Orleans power that road conditions through western Oklahoma were only going to worsen as the morning wore on. He wished again for the CB, thankful, at least, for the feel of the warm rubber pedals, the carpeted floorboard beneath his bare feet. Yet in spite of the creature comforts, Colter distrusted the delicate balance of the twelve-ton weight of his empty rig pulling against the shape of an icy curve. He didn't like what he felt as he feathered the accelerator pedal, and now, pushed for time with a hundred dark miles of snowpack and ice between here and Packingtown, he could sense the edge.

He drove on past a scatter of houses on the outskirts of Clinton, with their half dozen or so pole lights softened by the falling snow, on into the storm front, the snowfall heavier now, closing in around his headlight beams. And when Colter felt a faint tug on the wheel, then noticed the needle vibrating in a dashboard pressure gauge, he refused to believe it. Feeling immediately that old familiar sinking in his stomach, he glanced at the side mirror outside his open window where the trailer was supposed to be. Then in the next half second all hell broke loose, the image in his mirror swelling into distortion then disappearing again as the empty trailer fishtailed slowly back and forth across both lanes. Instinct took over as Colter feathered the accelerator and kept his hands off the tempting jake brake, but it took everything he had to keep the rig from jackknifing on the ice and rolling over. Slowly, finally, out near the end of a long eternity, the rig rocked to a stop, and for the second time in an hour Colter Wayne Tyree could feel the sure hand of fate cradling his life.

Chapter Four

Half expecting to hear the voice of God breaking in on the silent CB, Colter sat quietly for a moment and just shook, listening to the rough idle of the diesel and the slap of the windshield wipers while he marveled at the snow falling horizontally through the odd angle of his headlight beams.

Once clearheaded enough from the cold to choke off his panic, he slipped into his Nikes, and with Leon moaning in protest, stepped down from the running board onto the snowpacked, windblown surface of the highway. From the angle of the cab he could tell that his drivers were just off the shoulder of the pavement, but with chains and an empty box in back he might gain enough traction. So far, so good. Under the best of conditions Colter had always hated crawling around beneath all that weight, even for routine maintenance and safety checks. Now, at night, in the middle of a howling blizzard with the trailer listing at about thirty degrees off-center, the idea of wiggling down beneath all that dead-weight steel into the darker dark with nothing but a BIC lighter was absolutely terrifying.

Newer-model rigs had more sophisticated antilock braking systems, but with Colter's luck of the draw he knew the emergency braking system on this road-weary old ice box he was pulling had done exactly what it was designed to do. The jarring of an air line somewhere underneath the trailer, probably when he ran over that damn fool coyote, had resulted in a slow leak. Once the pressure dropped below a certain point the brakes had exploded into action, locking up the rear trailer duals like a vice. Colter couldn't imagine why the whole rig, empty and far too light for an icy road, hadn't simply flipped over and crushed him like a bug.

His hands shook with the thought of it, but he knew he was going to have to crawl down there in the mud and the snow and the dark and crank open the cocked valve on the air tank beneath the trailer and bleed off the line. If he could release the blown brakes and strap on the driver chains he could at least inch his way off the interstate. Five thirty-seven by his watch. First light in less than an hour, but Colter didn't need the light of day to tell him where he stood. He realized with the certainty of that same old sinking feeling that a load of swinging beef would wait for no man. And unless dispatch could find him another haul, he was looking at a lot of downtime while he waited out Easter weekend for somebody to repair the brakes and whatever else might have snapped in the fishtail. And he knew exactly where he'd be waiting. Knew the place by heart.

So, Colter Tyree was going home after all.

Coyote had spoken.

Chapter Five

"You can't bring that dog in here, Mister," the waitress said without turning around. Her contorted face shone in a chrome reflection off the coffee machine.

Colter couldn't tell if he was still shaking from the spinout or the cold sprint across the windswept street to the café. He stood with the door open, snow blowing in around his shoulders, muddy from head to foot and Leon at his side.

"Excuse me, Ma'am," he said, hat in hand, "but could you tell me what time does the station open up next door?"

The waitress looked up at the round-faced clock on the wall behind the counter that said 5:58.

"I don't even open for another two minutes," she said. "Kid supposed to be there by seven. He'll probably drag in with a hangover about a quarter to eight. Merle, guy owns the place, he went ice fishing with the lake froze over and all." She wore tortoiseshell glasses with sequins where the frames came out to a point. The glasses almost but not quite hid the little spiderweb wrinkles at the corners of her eyes. She had gathered her long, bleach-blonde hair into a high ponytail, and Colter thought she had a beaky kind of nose. She turned and eyed the two of them, her mouth moving in a frantic effort to completely demolish a stick of Juicy Fruit that Colter could smell from the door.

"I'll take the back booth," Colter said, glancing around the empty diner.

The place was spare and clean, with a lot of chrome showing behind the counter. Next to the cash register stood one of those little blue and white cardboard stands with a circle of red paper poppies for sale where the funds go to disabled vets. Colter noticed the only wall decorations in the place were a religious calendar with a picture of Jesus, arms outstretched like a cross and floating magically down the light rays as usual, and some Indian-looking thing with leather straps and feathers and a bone or two hanging off a framework of old barn wood. They hung side by side on the far left wall beside the back booth. He could feel the waitress looking at him as he took the place in.

"He'll lay down right at my feet," Colter said. "Anyone comes in, they won't even know he's here, okay? He just wants to sleep at my feet in the warm air. He's had a rough morning."

"That rough already, he sure must have gotten an early start." The waitress took a quick swipe at the spotless counter, popping that Juicy Fruit again inside her mouth. "Somebody'll be along. Bet on it. And when he comes in, you're going to have your hands full with that dog." She seemed to smile a little just saying it.

"Don't worry," Colter said, closing the door as quietly as possible behind him. Love me, love my dog, he said to himself. He wondered how long one little stick of Juicy Fruit could hold up under all that action. As he made his way along the short row of booths to the far back he could feel the warmth from the kitchen grill on his face.

"My daddy was a truck driver, the gypsy sonofabitch," the waitress joked, softening a little. "Mama, God rest her soul, she just never knew which one." She drew a cup of coffee from the tall, stainless steel urn, sliding the nearly full carafe out of the way and letting a small, dark stream run directly into Colter's cup, then deftly slipped the carafe back into the stream, letting only a drop or two pop and sizzle on the burner.

"We had a Lab once, I remember," she said, bringing the cup to the booth along with flatware wrapped in a napkin. "One of those black ones. I hadn't thought of that dog in years. Us kids always called him Snowflake for laughs," she said, looking from the dog to the snow blowing hard against the plate-glass window.

"Leon," Colter said, placing his high-crown Stetson just so on the seat beside him.

The waitress looked at him.

"The dog's name. Leon."

"Cute." The waitress brushed a loose strand of blonde hair out of her face and checked her wristwatch against the round-faced wall clock, and it looked to Colter like she was about to come back with something else when two coffee-colored clasped hands, bare arms, and a freckled brown face with high cheekbones and shining black hair appeared in the serving window that separated the kitchen area from the front of the café.

"White man gonna eat or just bullshit?" the apparition asked the waitress, looking suddenly at Colter. Then his face, lined as a beltway roadmap, broke into a wide, almost demented jack-o'-lantern grin with both lower front teeth missing.

He wore a red and black bandanna tied as a sweatband around his forehead. His thinning hair, mostly lost to forehead in front but still long in back and gathered low at the back of his neck, was dyed so black it looked purple in the shine of the fluorescent light from the kitchen. A great gold hoop dangled from his left ear. Colter knew immediately there was something familiar about the face, kind of a cross between an aging pirate and a clown. Something about those light gray eyes, though, the grin, and then Colter's heart sank, thinking suddenly of the river, of another lifetime a long time ago. And not wanting to go back there just now.

"Two eggs over medium, so the whites don't even wiggle," Colter said, going with the lighthearted flow of things. "Ham, browned a little around the edges, hash browns, but only if they're little chunks of real potato. I can't stand those stringy ones that come out of a pouch. Buttered toast, but I like to put my own butter on. Don't want it brushed out of a pot of melted butter you people scraped off somebody else's plate. Strawberry jelly, small tomato juice with a shaker of Tabasco on the side, and a toothpick with my meal. You get all that down, Ma'am?"

Colter had locked eyeballs with the crazy Indian cook and was determined not to blink first, even through his smile.

"Jesus," the waitress said, writing it all down on her pad.

"We melt the butter all right," said the Indian, "but I never thought of saving it off the plates. That's a good idea, Cole." He flashed his crazy grin again and waited while the waitress finished writing the ticket and pinned it with a clothespin to a wire stretched across the opening. As soon as she had pinned it the Indian reached up a long, bony hand, snatched it off with a practiced twang, and disappeared back into the kitchen. "You got to be Cole Tyree, right?" the Indian sang out invisibly from the kitchen. "I never forget a voice."

"Amazing." Thinking what a great name. Lonewolf. Oliver Lonewolf. First a lone wolf jumps up out of nowhere and dumps you against your will in your old hometown, then another Lonewolf pops up like a jack-in-the-box out of a roadside diner. Enough to make even a smart guy start to think in terms of omens.

"Oliver," Colter said simply.

"In the flesh, man. In the flesh and the spirit." Oliver peered out around the doorway wearing a black Grateful Dead T-shirt complete with skull, cobra, and a faded rose. "Ain't too many white eyes at a loss for words, huh Gladys?"

"I'm white, too," she said.

"Gladys, you got the soul of an Indian princess. A beautiful, brown soul trapped in that pale white body of yours."

Polite silence was all Colter could manage. Once a clown, always a clown. Oliver Lonewolf was certainly not your basic stoic wooden Indian. Way too much Irish for that.

"Oh, God," Gladys said, turning to Colter. "Cole Tyree . . . your daddy's the one . . ."

"Gladys!" the Indian said. "Cole, I never thought he was responsible."

Colter looked at the Indian's face in the doorway.

"Well, maybe that's not exactly true," Oliver said finally as he turned back into the kitchen. "At first maybe I blamed your daddy and everybody else in this town. Hell, your daddy *was* this town back then. But afterwards I knew it wasn't his fault. I just didn't want to believe my old man would do that to himself. Even if he wasn't *really* my old man. Thought he was too mean. Now, you know, I've seen some shit myself. Clearly be easier sometimes to just let go."

Colter nodded. "I think that same night killed my dad, too, you want to know the truth. Just took him longer to quit breathing."

"Your mom?" His head was again visible in the serving window with that same jack-in-the-box effect.

"Gone too. Suffered a stroke after the divorce. Finally died in a rest home out near us."

"Somebody said you lived out west now. Never knew just where."

"Albuquerque."

"She was a nice lady, your mom."

"Thank you for that."

"That's how I remember her," Oliver said. "Your grandma, too. As real nice ladies. Always ready with a peanut butter sandwich and a cold, sliced apple."

"Lighten up, okay?" The waitress glanced at the clock again. "This is beginning to sound awfully morose."

They both looked at her.

"Morose?" said the Indian. "Morose?"

"So, you been here all this time?" Colter asked, trying to get into it but having a very difficult time getting past the bandanna headband and gold hoop earring.

"Notice the headband?" the waitress said, turning to Colter. "He thinks since all us white folk surely want to be redskins, he has to be Jimi Hendrix."

"We invented headbands, Gladys. Christ, didn't you ever see *Broken Arrow* when you were a kid? The Lone Ranger and Tonto . . . just look at Tonto. And no, Cole, to answer your question, like about everybody else around here, I took a little time out for the Nam. But other than that, and one little spell where I was someplace else, I been right here."

"Roots," Colter said. The Nam talk made him immediately uncomfortable. He hoped to skip over the part about "everybody else around here."

"Yeah," the Indian said. "Roots."

"Someplace else?" said Gladys. "You took a little time out for ther-apy, you mean. Don't leave out that part. We met during therapy," she said, turning to Colter. "At the VA hospital in Oklahoma City. I wasn't in therapy, don't get me wrong. I worked in the cafeteria."

"And it was love at first sight, too. Right, babe?"

"He was a basket case. Full disability. Think he's bad now, that ear-ring and all, you should have seen him in therapy. Took role-playing right off the deep end. You can't imagine what he did in the war. And don't call me babe, Ollie."

"Don't call me Ollie, babe. And yeah, Cole, anybody can change. Look at me now; I'm a full-blood." Grinning ear to ear, that black gap where lower teeth should have been.

"As you can see, he still hasn't been fully rehabilitated," she said to Colter.

"Sounds like you two have forged a wonderful, caring relationship," Colter said. He was starting to feel trapped inside a cheap sitcom.

"And what did *you* do in Vietnam?" Gladys asked, her outpatient eavesdropping clearly a hard habit to break, but before Colter could begin to sweat out an answer the front door burst open, letting in another blast of late-winter cold.

Chapter Six

A powdering of snow blew out into the room, and out of the blast stepped a huge, grossly overweight man wearing a long, black wool overcoat. Hatless, with snowflakes clinging to a thick mane of dark brown hair only beginning to gray at the temples, the man swept a ham-sized paw from his low, squared-off brow line all the way back across his head, flinging drops of melt water onto the floor as he glanced around the diner.

The overcoat appeared expensive and finely made, out of place over the largest pair of faded blue denim overalls Colter had ever seen. Had to be special order, and the overalls were tucked into what looked like old knee-high jackboots. Oklahoma Highway Patrol boots. A little of the spit and polish gone, the boots a little worse for wear, but trooper boots just the same. Colter noticed that the Indian immediately disappeared back into the kitchen, away from the serving window.

The man was a giant. He stood well over six feet, ducking slightly when he came in the door, but height was only half the story. He was nearly as wide as the doorframe. He cleared the header easily but Colter could tell that ducking was an automatic mannerism, that the man had finally banged his head once too often and was now careful. He was hardly inside the door when he cast a glance around, touching Colter's eyes once lightly, then taking in the entire diner and lunch counter in one smooth sweep. He looked alert, agile, as if he could move very quickly in spite of his ridiculous size, and right away Colter felt an odd tension, almost as if he were trespassing. The waitress strangely offered no greeting. She immediately busied herself by drawing off a cup of hot water from the spigot on the side of the coffeemaker, keeping her distance behind the counter, as if she knew his moves.

"How's your boyfriend doing, sweetie?" the man asked, and it took Colter about half a second to place the softly spilling sound of the accent as deep coastal South, South Carolina maybe, or Georgia, the voice somehow too soft, too light to go with the man's size.

"He's fine, and thank y'all so very much for asking," she said, mimicking the accent. The words might have been playful banter, but something in the tone was all wrong.

"Sonofabitch is back there right now, isn't he? Hanging on to every word I say. Hey, boy, you back there listening?" He tried to raise his voice, turning with a grin to Colter for a reaction. "What you wearing today, Crazy Horse?" he went on. "Bet you're not wearing that breechcloth without your underpants today, are you now? That mangy dog hide keeping your ears warm this morning?"

"Why do you do it?" the waitress asked. "Why do you taunt him so? You wouldn't do this in earshot of a city councilman, would you?"

"Now you know better than that, Missy," he said, still smiling. "I'm under contract, you know. It's just that I can't seem to get used to one of our Noble Red Men of the Forest—and a crazy one at that—cohabiting with a decent white woman such as yourself. Guess I'm just kind of old fashioned that way."

Colter shifted uncomfortably in his seat. He had already begun to size the man up. Out of nowhere this conversation had burst upon him, and it made him very uncomfortable to watch anyone, let alone an old friend, be so shamed. He could feel his ears redden slightly, but he kept his seat, missing suddenly the solid weight of his little Smith & Wesson security blanket.

Leon had perked right up when the man came in. He lay at Colter's feet and growled a time or two, and each time Colter nudged him with his foot until the dog finally quit. But Leon didn't go back to sleep, and Colter reconciled himself to a tense breakfast, not knowing whether to worry more about the dog at his feet or the new player in a suddenly crowded game.

The man took a booth near the door, and the odd thing was that he sat down with his back to Colter. A little thing, but unusual, almost never done by a westerner, and it immediately made Colter even more uncomfortable. From the boots and the comments Colter thought the man had to be some kind of rent-a-cop. Retired highway patrol maybe, and yet there was something ludicrous about the image of a man his size trying to get in and out of a patrol car. All his clothes, even the boots, would have to be special order stuff. The boots alone would probably weigh fifteen pounds. They couldn't be comfortable, and they'd be hell to polish. No, he thought, this guy wears them because he likes the way he looks in them. No visible badge, but Colter also noticed what looked like the bulge of a sidearm beneath the dark sweep of overcoat as the man turned away to sit down. Rent-a-cop maybe, or nightwatchman. That was it. Colter hadn't thought of the term "nightwatchman" since he left home. In the larger, outside world the guy would be a security guard. He had to be the town nightwatchman, maybe just coming off his shift. Rural RoboCop.

Colter noticed that Oliver hadn't returned his face to the serving window. The waitress had begun preparing a cup of hot Lipton tea from a box on the counter, placing the bag in the cup just so, with the string tag hanging out opposite the cup handle, and pouring the hot water as soon as the man came in the door. Now that the man had settled into the booth she brought it to him. He neither thanked her nor even nodded as she silently placed the saucer and a half dozen creamers on the Formica and retreated behind the counter. Colter could hear the man's spoon tinkle, bell-like, inside the thick white china cup while he added both sugar and cream and stirred the mix cool.

"I'll go on and take my breakfast now, Missy," he said.

His voice was definitely a notch higher pitched than his size suggested, with an almost musical softness to it.

"Six over easy, toast and hash browns, twice ham," she called out to the kitchen. The Indian still hadn't shown himself.

"No, Missy, you don't mind, I'd like you to cook them eggs yourself this time."

Colter couldn't believe his ears.

"Showing off a little this morning, are we officer? It's all right. Nothing too good for an officer of the law," she said, and disappeared into the kitchen without so much as a glance in Colter's direction.

After she had gone the man turned just enough in his booth to indicate he might be talking to Colter, and said, "Had a nigger cook poison a fella once, back where I'm from, so I seldom let a colored cook for me."

That was all he said, and he said it as if he owed Colter some kind of explanation, but the man's Deep South accent said it all.

"Another dog missing," the nightwatchman said, making conversation in a louder voice while he waited on his eggs. "You hear that, Crazy Horse?"

Gladys stayed in the back.

"Dogs are missing?" Colter said. Someone dropped a pan with a clatter onto the kitchen floor in back and Colter wished immediately he had kept still.

"Travel with that dog do you, Bud?" said the nightwatchman, turning awkwardly again in the booth.

"Old Leon," Colter said, wishing again he had kept his mouth shut. "Been with me so long I just don't have the heart to turn him out."

"Stick around here, you won't have to. I got a notion some of these renegade Cheyenne are eating 'em."

No one said anything at all to that. The conversation was over, and when Gladys brought out the food and returned immediately to the kitchen, they both ate in silence, Colter staring up occasionally at the unkempt wedge of hair hanging over the collar of the nightwatchman's long, black overcoat.

"By the way, son," the nightwatchman finally said, leaning around in the booth again, "you got something leaking out into a puddle underneath that trailer. Looked like maybe coming from a hydraulic line or something. I didn't look underneath, but that's what she looks like to me."

"Shit," Colter said, trying against his will to accommodate polite conversation. "Knew I'd blown the air line to the lock-ups soon as the fool things locked up. Sure didn't know about any hydraulics, though. Ran over a damn coyote out on the interstate," he said, immediately feeling a traitor for cursing the coyote and conversing in such friendly hillbilly tones with his old friend's certain enemy. And "son." What was this "son" crap? Some crude attempt at authority? Colter could hear an alarm bell inside his head.

"Well, well," the nightwatchman said louder. "You hear that, Crazy Horse? Fella here ran over your cousin."

When there was no response from the kitchen, the man turned full around to the side, swinging his huge thighs out into the room, and looked at Colter out of eyes of the strangest, lightest blue.

"Coyotes been coming into town after dark lately," he said. "Mostly just raiding trash cans, but yesterday Clara Nelson's little poodle come up missing. Guess she turned him out to pee and the little squirt never came back in."

Leon growled again, but he quit at Colter's nudging.

The nightwatchman looked down at the dog. "You going to stick around to fix the brakes and all, you might want to lock up your dog in the truck. I've heard him growl a time or two since I came in, and this is, after all, an eating establishment of sorts. If that crazy savage in the kitchen doesn't put him in the soup pot, I might have to shoot him. If he were to get loose, you understand, come at me or something. It seems I am, along with other official designations, the animal control officer for this fine little metropolis. Understood?"

Colter's heart pounded in his throat. He could feel his palms begin to sweat from the adrenaline rush, and all he could do was nod agreement while he tried to imagine what size casket it would take to hold the bastard. They finished their breakfast in awkward silence, Colter picturing the two proprietors huddled in the back, one of them armed to the teeth and waiting while they all listened to the distinct sounds of chewing, the occasional clink of flatware against thick café china.

Chapter Seven

As soon as the giant had finished his tea and eggs, leaving a five-dollar bill on the Formica, he lumbered his way out of the diner without so much as a word to anyone, ducking again as he cleared the doorframe. With the solid click of the door latch the Indian's clown face appeared again in the serving window, minus the grin.

"What the hell was that all about?" Colter asked.

"You don't even want to know," Oliver said. "I don't have a clue where the town fathers found that one. Sonofabitch. He hunts your granddaddy's old place, Cole. That old creek bottom hasn't been cleared in years. What with your daddy not that interested in keeping up the place toward the end, the bottom is pretty well gone to scrub. Our John Law there, he's probably headed out right now to blast him another coyote. I see him when I walk around sometimes."

"He hunts the place?"

"Coyotes. Sometimes hangs the carcasses off a fence post, but mostly he just lets 'em lay where they fall. Too fucking lazy to even clean up after himself. No hide, no bounty, no reason. Just likes to kill things. He's robbing graves, too. Indian graves. I know he's doing it, and he knows I know. Remember those old graves in that plum thicket up along the east side of your granddaddy's place, up there beside the tracks? Well, I've seen the holes he's dug in there. Sonofabitch is selling off burial offerings to collectors, but I can't prove it yet. And him the law, too. This fucking place is incredible. You're lucky to be long gone."

"He makes my skin crawl, too," Gladys said, "but I still wish you'd clean up your language."

"I learned to talk in Vietnam, Gladys. I learned a lot of other things there, too. Sharpened a few other skills. Isn't it wonderful that my language skills are the only ones I've managed to retain."

"Small favor," she said.

"Anytime he comes in, Cole, I'm here, I grab a butcher knife and stay in the back. Someday I'll probably have to kill the motherfucker."

"Ollie!"

"Ollie my ass, Gladys. He ever comes through the door into the kitchen, he's mine. Next time you see him, he's in somebody's flame-broiled burger."

"Where'd they find him?" Colter asked. "Is he really some kind of law?"

"Nightwatchman," said Oliver. "He's only the nightwatchman, for chrissake. You'd think he was Commanding General of the Armies of the Republic instead of a goddamn glorified dog catcher."

"He's creepy," the waitress said. "Josie Magpie, she cleans for the motel, she says he pretty much lives out of a suitcase and a big trunk in number seven on the end."

"Has gun, well traveled," Oliver said. "The town fathers hired him on contract about six months ago to patrol the town at night. What he does is sneak off and dig up dead Indians or harass us live ones. Sleeps in his pickup all night on Main Street, calls it work, and then shoots coyotes all day."

"He's a joke, all right," Colter said, "but he's sure not very funny."

"Drives one of those four-wheel-drive monster trucks. You know, the kind with a carbine on a rack in the back window and running lights across the top of the cab, mud flaps. Shoot, it's even got an honest-to-God red flashing gumball machine and a megaphone built in. All your regular law and order bullshit, only his is one of those little miniature Toyotas. You ought to see it. Probably had to modify the cab just to shoehorn the fat motherfucker's ass into the seat."

"There's that word again," Gladys said. "Take your pill this morning?"

"I think I'll just sit here quietly now and finish my coffee and hope the kid next door can fix my brakes in a hurry," said Colter. "I stick around here, I'm clearly going to have a problem with him. Is he really fooling around Dad's old place?"

"You mean your place, don't you? And yeah, he is. 'No trespassing' doesn't apply to the law. And yeah, you'll have a problem all right," the Indian said. "You stick around, you'll have a problem. He didn't pay you much mind because he thinks you're just a driver pulled in off the interstate."

"That's exactly what I am," Colter said. "Consider me a driver just pulled in off the interstate. I didn't figure on seeing anyone I knew anyway. Least of all Cochise here," he said to Gladys with a smile.

"Crazy Horse," Oliver said. "It's Crazy Horse. Don't you know, man? Cochise was actually a figment of the collective Hollywood imagination. Some honky in Maybelline. Crazy Horse was a fucking saint. Bulletproof, too. They finally had to knife him. A martyr who died for your sins, white man."

"Ollie!"

"My sins?" Colter said.

"The sins of the father, in your case," said Oliver.

"Ollie!"

"Joke," the Indian said, sticking his head out of the serving window again. "Bad joke. Sorry. And I told you, Gladys, don't call me Ollie. My name is Oliver Wendell Crazy Horse fucking Lonewolf. You may both refer to me as Crazy Horse, but please, with more respect in your voice than our large, absent friend."

"How about just Crazy, Mr. Horse?" Gladys said. "And we did forget our pill this morning, didn't we?"

"Crazy Horse," Oliver said, ducking back into the kitchen.

"Horse's ass," Gladys said quietly to Colter, "and he did forget his pill. I can always tell."

"And Johnny?" Colter asked. He remembered when Johnny, Oliver's brother, ran off and joined the navy.

"Never came back," Oliver said from the kitchen. "But then, what's a brother for, I always say. Sorry motherfucker."

"He been like this long?" asked Colter.

"Don't patronize me, Cole, goddamnit," the Indian said from somewhere in the kitchen, his voice carrying above the noisy banging of pots and pans. "You're born, raised here, from kin been here, what, three generations, you go away for thirty years or better, and then one day you pop in, you don't figure on seeing anyone you know? Come on. I'm just a shell-shocked Cheyenne running around like a fool in my underwear now and then, but I ain't exactly stupid. You either came here to see somebody or be seen by somebody. Praise or absolution, who knows, but you came for something."

"I ran over a coyote," Colter said. Again.

Oliver stuck his head back out through the serving window, that jack-in-the-box image again.

"I ran over a coyote, that's all. Didn't mean to. Poor fool just came out of nowhere in the middle of a little nap I was taking at the wheel and saved my life or I'd be out there dead right now with forty feet of steel wrapped around my head. That's why I stopped. When the brakes blew on me, this was the next exit."

"In this storm?" Oliver asked. "What was a coyote doing out in the middle of the night in a snowstorm? They got better sense."

Colter shrugged. "Storm's not that bad farther west. Took a while for the brakes to go. Anyway, I told you. He came out specifically to save my ass. I dozed off. Woke up when I hit him. Clearly there is a greater purpose to my life than I have yet realized."

"Clearly," said Gladys.

"Now, Gladys," Oliver said. "Don't get out your crystals."

"Smart aleck. There is a master plan, you know. We're all part of it."

"Leon sure didn't like him," Colter said, trying to steer the conversation away from crystals and master plans.

"Animals are smarter that way," the Indian said. "And speaking of dogs, he wasn't kidding."

Oliver came out through the swinging door from the kitchen, all six thin feet of him, and came right over to Colter's booth. "Hey, pup," he said, stooping down and offering the back of his hand for Leon to sniff. Leon obliged, slapping Colter's ankles with his tail, then allowed his ears to be scratched. "There have been a couple come up missing, all right," he said, straightening up. "But I don't think it's coyotes. I've actually watched that asshole use a stray dog for target practice.

"Sonofabitch pulled up one time at the end of the alley behind J & E Grocery, spotted an old stray blue heeler bitch sniffing around the trash cans, you know, trying to find food for her pups. Just stuck that .30–30 of his out the window and 'boom.' One shot from the end of the alley. Echo rattled all the backroom windows on the block, and when I stuck my head out the back door of the pool hall and asked him about it, he just said he was doing his job, that's all. 'Indian dog,' he said. Made a joke out of offering the carcass to me for soup meat. Been on my ass ever since."

"He's just afraid of us because we live . . . differently," Gladys said.

Colter waited for more. There had to be more.

"Because we live off the land," Gladys said.

"We don't live off the land, Gladys," Oliver said, turning back toward the kitchen. "You don't have any real concept of what it's like to live off the land. Someday I will tell you what living off the land is all about. But living off the land is not what we do."

"Well, pardon me, Mr. Horse."

"I lived off the land a time or two in the Nam, all right. Come to think of it, I actually ate dog once in a very exclusive Saigon restaurant. Here I do not eat dog."

"But we do live in a teepee," Gladys said. "At least in the summer. That's what I mean. He's afraid of us because we live differently than most people."

"No offense, Ma'am," said Colter, "but he didn't look exactly scared shitless." Then, to Oliver, who had disappeared again into the kitchen, "So, you live in a tent, huh?"

"A teepee," said Oliver. "Pitched it on tribal land over by the lake so those social service creeps would leave us alone. Army surplus canvas instead of stitched buffalo hide, but a teepee, you know, stretched over poplar poles. Couldn't get any good, straight lodgepole pine around here. Got us a little Airstream, too, for winter. Silver bullet, just like the Lone Ranger. Twenty-two footer with tandem axles. Don't own anything to pull her with, so I got her sittin' up on blocks with the tires stored out of the sun. Never know when you'll have to roll; you want good tires. So, you live in a house, do you, Bud?"

Colter had to think about that one.

"Well, I sort of live out of a truck right now. My wife lives in my house. Our house. At least it used to be our house." Somehow Colter hoped it sounded worse than it really was. He made a mental note to use the pay phone outside as soon as he left the diner. Looked at that way, it was clear that he and Marilyn didn't even share a house anymore, let alone a life.

"I move around a lot, too," Oliver said. "On a slightly smaller scale."

Colter and Gladys shared a glance.

"Oliver likes to walk. He patrols," Gladys said.

"No big deal," Oliver said. "I came back, you know, from the Nam, and it was like I missed it. You know what I mean. Not the action so much, like the rest of the crazies. Just the woods. Humping the boonies. All us redskins grew up in the woods, you know that. Boiled spring water until we got a well with a cast-iron hand pump out in the yard, that kind of thing. Shoot, I bet you remember Myrtle's old place, that outhouse in back. It's still there, by the way. The outhouse. Still in daily use, too. So the Nam wasn't any great big thing to me. Just more woods. So hey, I came back home, and it just seemed natural to range out into the woods again. Only here the woods are safe. Took me a while to get used to that, all right."

"About thirty years and the clock's still ticking," said Gladys.

"I was a little stressed out, okay? I knew guys came home a lot worse off. Bunch of my buddies got boxed up prior to shipment. Someday I'm gonna go run my finger over their names at that memorial, too. Drink a beer 'n' shed a tear. So, Cole, what'd you do in-country?"

There was that question again, and this time Colter could think of no way to avoid it. In all his long and uneventful life, Colter Wayne

Tyree had only once heard a shot fired in anger. It was a long time ago, and they weren't shooting at him. Coming of age during Vietnam, noncombatant status was his great shame, but he stood his ground, made up some nonsense about being a rear echelon company officer without saying how far to the rear, and asked back quickly, discovering that Oliver had gone to war white and had come home Indian.

With both his Indian mother and his grandfather long since dead, and Oliver left alone at the very outside edge of any tribal connection as a red-haired, freckled, half-breed, high school dropout after the death of his stepfather, the "last in a long line of sorry white men," he was eventually taken in as a "troubled youth" by a white family over by Tulsa. That much Colter remembered. Within a couple of years he apparently graduated high school, but with conforming way down on his skills list and facing the relentless lottery of the draft like everybody else, he had volunteered. Not just to join up, either. Apparently bought the whole package from some fast-talking recruiter and went for Airborne, Ranger training, and Officer Candidate School, in those days a quick ticket to cannon fodder. Ended up a Forward Observer and glorified mud grunt, calling in air strikes for an infantry company in the Mekong Delta. First month in-country he traded a shrapnel hit from a claymore booby trap for a Purple Heart, and when he came home, pretty sure by then that his white half was losing ground fast, it was to Fairview and his thin tribal connections. Easier, he said, to be just another drunk Indian. Same old, same old, though, and when his med leave was up he volunteered for a second tour, this time with Special Forces, and even cycled through the Special Warfare School at Bragg while Colter was freeloading as a training officer, although they never ran into each other. Bottom line, according to Gladys, Oliver was so good with a long gun and a scope they made him a fucking assassin. Amazing if it was all true. According to enthusiastic Gladys he apparently went native on them, passing himself off as the tallest Montagnard tribesman in the history of the world and stalking around the jungle picking off VC brass on assignment. When Nixon shut her down and Oliver offered to hang around strictly freelance on a kind of piecework basis they bundled him up in a straightjacket and sent him home again, this time for a stint as an outpatient with the VA.

Colter couldn't be sure whether the whole thing was true, or if they both had been watching too many reruns of a certain Oliver Stone movie, but apparently after a few rough years flirting with AIM and the Red Power Movement, he had sobered up long enough to join a newly formed all-Indian AA chapter. Later, at the vo-tech school over at Okmulgee, far from his old, hard-drinking Cheyenne buddies, he had learned the cooking trade. Colter couldn't imagine the difficulty of such a climb up out of the hole. With a white-trash stepfather who beat him and a brother who ran away from home and a mother who died too young, Oliver had apparently fought long and hard to stay out of the quicksand of alcohol and violence that claimed most of the Cheyenne in and around Fairview. His favorite cafeteria waitress, divorced now and clearly along for more than just the ride, had graduated to outpatient counselor.

Oliver must have something going for him, Colter thought. Maybe it was just those long, bony hands, but whatever it was, one thing led to another and here the man was, right back where he started. Roots.

By the time Colter left a tip, grabbed a pack of Juicy Fruit for dessert, and paid his tab it was nearly eight. When he and Leon left the café and headed back out into the storm the wind had not dropped even a little, the snowflakes were like tiny airborne icicles as they swirled around the street lamps, and Colter had to hold his hat on. He didn't want to encounter the nightwatchman again. Ever. The man would clearly be a handful. Imagining a flood of very real consequences, Colter could sense the edge again. What do I care if the guy digs a few holes out at the old Tyree place, he thought. Sure ain't Tyree bones the guy's digging up.

He was beginning to feel like a Stranger in a Strange Land. "Beam me up, Scotty," he said aloud, his voice lost quickly in the wind.

Chapter Eight

The biting wind tearing across the filling station drive actually felt good again after the closeness of the diner. It was as if the nightwatchman had somehow used up all the air inside.

With the station owner off ice fishing at the lake, the boy running the place, no fool, had left the little space heater in the office going all night, so the front of the station was almost as warm as the diner. Even had the same Jesus calendar on the wall behind the cash register, alongside a poster of some blonde Amazon with huge boobs selling shock absorbers and brake pads. The kid had left the inside door into the garage bays open, too, so that a spillover of warm air would take the chill off the work area, but the boy was definitely alone, and Colter knew immediately that getting anything done in a hurry was out of the question. He wished again the whole thing had never happened.

"Gonna be later this morning before I can even look at it," the boy said after Colter filled him in on the high points. He nodded his pimpled face helplessly toward the garage bays. Each bay harbored a pickup truck, one already raised into the air on the smooth, silver column of the hoist for some undercarriage work, the other immobilized on the floor with its hood open like a waiting dental patient. Work is long, Colter thought to himself. Life is short. The boy wore a bandanna tied around his head in the same Karate Kid manner as Colter's cheerful friend next door. Something in the water, maybe. Too much rural fluoride.

"Ten, maybe? You think by ten?"

The boy shrugged again. "Can't do much out there on the drive until it warms up, you know."

"Yeah," Colter said. "That's true." He looked out across the drive, the hardened snowpack scoured clean by the wind, the sky gray now as concrete, and he couldn't immediately remember a colder, more hopeless scene than the cold, dead metal of his own tractor-trailer rig. Stuck here, of all the hopeless little towns in the wide world, after all those years avoiding the place like the plague.

"How about I jockey her in a little closer, maybe back the rear axle in under the driveway overhang. That help?"

"Naw," the boy said. "Might make it a little easier, closer to the tools and all, but it'll block the drive. Boss wants me to sell that gas, you know."

"Sure. You bet." He wondered idly who among his many old friends might have fathered, perhaps mothered, this genius. Hopefully no McRae in him.

Now where did that come from, he wondered. God, he hadn't thought of her since the last time he roared past on the interstate.

"Any new motels hereabouts?" He could feel himself falling under the spell of the place again. "Hereabouts?" Jesus. He could hear the old speech patterns shooting straight from his brain right out into the air like he'd never been gone at all. And it was so easy . . . you bet, y'all, jes like fallin' off a log somewheres . . . got a motel hereabouts . . . Maybe that's what going home means, he thought. Why we avoid it. Like sinking back into quicksand.

"Naw. Got one, but it's full of by-the-weekers. Got a old hotel, though. They maybe got a room. It's where all the weeklies moved out from when they built the motel. Two weird ladies gonna do a bed or breakfast with it. Something like that. Storm keeps up, they'll be puttin' tourists up in the gym. Seen it happen. Want me to call?"

The boy was waiting for him to decide, but there wasn't much to decide.

"I'll stop by. Gonna run out by the cemetery anyway." He was sorry as soon as he said it.

"No shit. In this weather?" the kid said, showing a sudden interest. "You got kin here?"

There it was again. Another golden opportunity for truth come knocking. Own up or soft-shoe, what'll it be? "Long time ago," he said. Colter could already hear the jungle drums.

"What's your name, Mister, don't mind my askin'?"

"Tyree. Last name's Tyree."

The boy thought a moment. "Nope," he said. "Never heard of you."

Colter took another breath, thinking the alternative to this crap was to inch his way on down the back roads, through Watonga and Kingfisher and Okarche, knowing he wouldn't be able to get any help until he reached the city. Take him the better part of the rest of his life to reach the city in this weather anyway, and by that time he and the dog both would have starved to death or died of boredom in the cab. At least it felt good to be outside and moving around for a change. And legitimately, too. The storm was as good as a note from his mother.

"So, where do you want her then?" he asked, getting off the subject of the cemetery and his obviously famous name.

"Just jackknife in alongside the building here." The boy nodded toward the lee side. "Might leave room enough there for folks to get into the restrooms. Being on the south side, it'll get the sun when this blows out."

What, a week or two, Colter thought to himself, mentally wincing at the term "jackknife."

The boy looked at him as if he could read minds. "Couple days maybe. Radio said it was blowing out all across the state. 'Course parts is a whole 'nother issue. Ain't no parts houses gonna open till Monday anyway, if it needs something. Weatherman on the radio said they was another front coming in behind this one, too, but he said it don't have no moisture in it. Said something about a cold air mass. Something like that. Ask me, the sun'll be out by tomorrow afternoon."

The visible sky, white and featureless through the station windows, gave no hint of clearing.

"What the hell," Colter said, resignation creeping into his voice. The false high of the coffee was wearing off, and he could feel the hours and the miles and the adrenaline damage deep down in his bones. He had wanted to unhook the tractor anyway while the boy worked on the trailer, maybe take a quick spin through the old hometown, take a look at the lake, stop by the cemetery for a quick look at the old man's grave, then head out onto the road again, grab his load in Oklahoma City by nightfall. Not going to happen. Good weather and they might have sent him on his way to deadhead the tractor, pick up another loaded trailer waiting somewhere within a two- or three-hundred-mile radius. Dispatch would simply have sent another driver to grab the trailer when the brakes were fixed. Now he was going to have to call in with a delay, something he wasn't looking forward to at all.

Worst of it, he knew he was going to have to call home.

Chapter Nine

What had to be the very last telephone booth in the world stood out next to the street where the wind really whipped across the driveway. Snow pelted his face as he pushed open the door and stepped inside. Under normal circumstances Colter Tyree could no longer close the door to a telephone booth. The space was too tight even with see-through walls, but this morning, with the wind raging across the drive at gusts of probably forty or better, the inside of a telephone booth felt pretty good. The wind blasted at his legs and feet but the shelter of the glass felt good, secure, and he marveled at the way the snow came at the glass straight-out level, all the way down from Kansas. Amazing, too, to find the telephone book, thin as it was, still attached to the booth. Nothing like a small town, he thought.

Tough stuff first. Always sounded like such a good rule, Colter thought he'd try it once. He tipped his hat back and dialed the charge code, the area code, and his home number, the black telephone cold against his ear. Marilyn picked up on the second ring.

"That was quick," he said. Around eight in the morning here, so seven there. "You sound wide awake."

"I am," she said. A silence.

"I'm fine," he volunteered. "Truck's not so fine, but I'm fine."

There was another awkward silence, then she said, "What happened to the truck that you're calling me at seven in the morning? This better not be an April Fool's joke. Not after last night."

"No wreck," he said. "No wreck." Christ, he hadn't even thought about April Fool's Day. He could hear her breath start up again on the other end. "It's not a joke, though. I hit a coyote. At least I think it was a coyote. Busted an air line. Looks like the trailer might have a little downtime. Maybe I should fly home for the weekend."

Silence.

"Be down a day or two, anyway. They'll probably have to send to the city for parts. Saturday, Easter weekend and all, it'll probably be Monday before they get anything out here."

"Where's here?" she asked.

Now it was his turn for a second of silence. He tried to regroup but it was too late. "Fairview. I'm in Fairview," he said, and it sounded strange to say it.

"You're telling me you're in Fairview? Oklahoma?"

"Yup," he said. "I'm home," which sounded stranger yet.

"Are you okay?" she asked again. "You don't sound so okay . . ."

"I'm fine. Promise. I didn't even know anything broke until I stopped for coffee at this little diner out here by the interstate. Old friend of mine runs it. A night cop coming off duty spotted the leak." In Colter's book, a half-truth was better than no truth at all, which meant he felt fine skipping the part where his brakes locked up. "And boy is the night cop a whole other story."

"How's the mutt?" she asked, skipping the other story.

"Fine. Asleep at the moment. He does a lot of that. I'm sorry," he said.

Silence again.

"I said I'm sorry," he repeated. "The supper last night, the wine, all wonderful. I really am sorry."

"I heard you and yes you are sorry. You're a sorry ass to go off like that."

"Well, you can't just start a fight like that just before it's time to leave. Because then I have to leave and nothing gets finished."

"Nothing gets finished anyway," she said. "I hate your truck. I hate your leaving. I hate your life. You could find something . . ."

"I'm sorry," he said again. God, how he had dreaded this call.

"I mean, I make enough for both of us. Until you could find something else . . ." Another silence. Then, "You sure you're okay? I mean why there, of all places?"

"You said that already. Why anyplace? This doesn't have to be any different than anyplace else, does it? I mean, it's not like I was exiled or something. It's my hometown, for chrissake. I ought to be able to come here any time I want."

"You can," she said. "You always could. But we can discuss it later. Sometime after seven in the morning. Just so you're okay."

"I'm okay. Really. Roads are bad, but I could probably dead-head into the city. Maybe catch a flight out this afternoon," realizing instantly the flight would have to go on her Visa card.

Another pause, then, "Actually, I'm stuck with an out-of-town client all weekend. You were leaving anyway, so I took floor this afternoon for Todd. It'll give me a chance to get ready before the Williamsons fly in this evening from Denver. Call me again tomorrow, though, okay?"

"Sure," he said, sensing the coming end of the conversation, but there was something about that last pause that bothered him. Then there was the part about "call me tomorrow." Not tonight. Colter began to sense that the machinery for his replacement might already be in motion. So much for flying home for a passionate Easter reconciliation.

"Call me, okay? Do you want me to wire you some money?"

"No. Christ no. Don't send money."

Silence again.

"Sorry. I don't need your money, okay? Sorry. I am sorry. I wish I could just turn around and come home tonight. Make it right, you know?"

"Just call me tomorrow, then. Okay? And as long as you're there, take something out to the cemetery, too. You've put that off way too long. Love and kisses."

"I love you too," he said, but not quickly enough to beat the "gotta go now" and click on the other end. He replaced the phone, the black Lucite finally warm to his touch, and felt a little pissed, as usual, at her brisk efficiency on the telephone. Another control issue to be discussed. But, like she had said, later. Always later. He decided immediately he wouldn't call tomorrow. And he was going to run out to the cemetery anyway, thank you. Exercise a little control of his own.

At least he had done his part. Nothing resolved, of course, but except for the money part, he felt better. Jesus. How she needed him to be needy. He had apologized, and he really had truly wanted to fly home. That would surely be worth something in the Final Ledger. Suddenly wondering what Rae Lynn's last name was now. Whether she still lived in the area. Jesus. Whether she was even still alive.

Always faithful as a collie pup on the road in spite of the falling-apart nature of the marriage, Colter didn't need any of that shit welling up just now. He felt more than a little conflicted, torn between hoping to accidentally run into Rae Lynn McRae, or whatever her name might be now, and hoping not to. The call home hadn't helped.

The call to the dispatcher didn't turn out any better.

Chapter Ten

"Colter Tyree, number 227, deadheading east, calling dispatch," he said to the switchboard girl.

"Hold a moment," she said as always, leaving off the "please."

He hated to call in. He always hated to call in, but he especially hated to call in Easter weekend, broken down in some Podunk town in western Oklahoma that just happened to be his hometown. It made him want that note from his mother after all. He waited for which-ever unpleasant voice would come on the line next. Turned out to be Charley Neary, very close to a worst-case scenario.

"Deadhead, you say? Where's the fucking trailer?"

"Hello, Charley. I'm fine. Don't worry about me. I'm okay."

"Where you calling from, hotshot?"

No pleasantries, no how you doing, are things going well for you, our trusted, valuable employee, no nothing. Just where's the fucking trailer. Someday soon Colter knew he was going to quit. Someday real soon. Before he killed himself in some accident, cooked inside his own oven, or before he strangled somebody from dispatch with his bare hands.

"Oklahoma, Charley," he said. "I-40, mile marker 132 out of Okie City."

There was a brief silence while Charley calculated where Colter should have been, and then he said, "This better not be some fucking April Fool joke. Joke'll be on you. What's the trouble?"

An obvious problem here, trying to tell anybody anything important on April first. "Brake line coming out of the rear slave. Had a damn coyote run right into it." He noticed, too, that blaming the damn coyote was getting easier each time. No mention this time of his mystical salvation at the hands of a cleverly disguised angel.

"Ha, looks like the coyote finally put the brakes on the roadrunner," Charley said, pleased at the quickness of his own joke.

"Right now it looks about even," he said, thinking again about the coyote. "Kid at the station said with the weather it'd be late Saturday before they could get parts out of the city. If then. Storm's pretty much shut down western Oklahoma. So can you get me a load anywhere? Let somebody else nab the beef? With chains I can get the tractor back on the road. Weather's tracking southeast, so how about a flatbed load out of Dallas to anywhere while I leave the reefer here for the kid to work on? How about that?"

"Mile marker 132, huh?" Charley said.

Colter waited for it. Charley had driven a million, million miles in the last years before they retired him to dispatch. He seemed to have the entire USA permanently imprinted in one of those tiny trenches in the front of his brain. He could probably visualize the countryside around the exit, might even know where the telephone booth stood, but Colter doubted he had all the personnel files memorized too.

"That'd put you out around Oakwood . . . maybe Fairview . . . right?"

Amazing. More than a little scary. "Right, Charley. Right on target. Fairview. How do you do it?" Colter figuring a little stroking right about now might sidetrack things.

"Shit, Mr. Colter Tyree," Charley said, "I know where you are better than you know most of the time. You know . . ."

"Sure enough. You bet. Listen, Charley," Colter broke in, mission accomplished, "the wind's whipping in under this telephone booth, climbing up my pants legs and freezing my ass off like I was wearing a grass skirt. Can you get me anything? Anything at all? I told you, I'll even take a flatbed with a canvas tie-down. How's that for easy?"

"Monday."

"Monday? Don't talk to me about Monday, Charley. I can't hang around this little burg the whole weekend. Jesus. I want to hear sometime today."

"Monday. If they can't get the part today, nobody's going to do anything until Monday morning anyway. That's a single-user beef contract. No splits. Single-destination user. Already in cold storage, and the way the weather sounds, it's probably not going to thaw by Monday. You get out of there by noon Monday, you can easy make St. Louie by midnight, Okie City drop and all. This is Easter weekend, Mr. Tyree, in a Methodist state to boot. You're not going to get shit done until sometime Monday. I'll let 'em know in Louie, and you let me know the minute that van's ready to roll. Right? You can't roll by noon Monday, we'll talk flatbed."

"Sure. Gotcha, boss."

"And forward those receipts, too. From last week. You're already backed up again. It's getting to be a habit, you know? It's attracting attention."

With my bare hands, Colter was thinking. Instead, he said, "*Sí, sí, señor. Gracias y adios,*" all in his best taco accent, and hung up. At least he wouldn't lose the load over it. At least that.

Colter had to acknowledge his attitude was getting to be a problem. He also knew that much more downtime would cost him dearly. Flatbed cowboys were a dime a dozen, all of them just waiting for a reefer opening, and he could tell he wasn't exactly management's fair-haired boy anymore. Bad enough that Marilyn had to quit teaching just to cover the losses from his little entrepreneurial fiasco. Worse yet she was succeeding so well selling fancy houses that she could easily wire him money out on the road. But if he lost enough time behind the wheel to put the tractor payments in jeopardy, he could see himself becoming completely irrelevant. Truth be known, he felt that way most of the time anyway.

He needed a little homestay, no doubt about it. But just now he needed to be on the road again, pulling that reefer van full of meat hooks and dead cows over to St. Louis. Be the last hurrah if he couldn't make his tractor payment. Despite the growing claustrophobia, he thought he could probably hang on as a solo driver with at least an illusion of independence. But past fifty now, with a geriatric Labrador in tow, Colter Tyree couldn't imagine hiring on as a galley slave again, replacing the Lab with some flatulent, tobacco-chewing, cowboy-boot-wearing, depressed, alcoholic mirror image of himself, whose troubles he'd have to listen to in that tiny box a million miles at a time. Better to just shuffle into the nearest Wal-Mart, hire on as a greeter, and wait out the count.

Blame it on the weather, he thought, facing that horizontal snow outside the booth again while he held on to his once-upon-a-time two-hundred-dollar Stetson with a death grip. Road slick as owl shit, no brakes, twenty-some thousand pounds of welded steel riding a foot behind your neck, what's a guy to do.

He had left the diesel engine idling, and with his emergency flashers and all the running lights still on, the rig looked just like it always did after a quick pit stop: rearing to go. Stepping slowly up onto the running board, feeling that momentary hesitation at climbing into the tiny cab, and thinking again of the violent pounding the poor coyote must have taken to do so much damage in so little time, he noticed the nightwatchman's pickup still parked just behind the diner with only the hood, windshield, and rooftop bank of chrome spots visible around the diner corner.

With the pickup motor running and the front windshield fogged over, Colter couldn't see inside but he had the distinct and immediate impression he was being observed. Well, let the sonofabitch watch, he thought, refusing to get dragged into something there.

Leon whined his usual, arthritic whine as Colter helped him up into the door, but once in the shotgun seat he flopped comfortably a time or two, passed a little gas, and before Colter finished checking the dash gauges (oil pressure great, air pressure in the lock-ups non-existent) the dog was fast asleep. Colter slowly released the brakes on the tractor, now the only brakes for the entire unit, and it went against all his driver's instincts to move the rig one single foot without every-thing working properly. He started to back around slowly, position-ing the trailer so the filling station attendant could get to it, and with the first halting movement of the trailer, the nightwatchman stepped out of his pickup to watch. A difficult operation at best, and now the stupid nightwatchman has to stand out in the blizzard and supervise, Colter thought, making a mental note and filing it under the category: Assholes I've Run Into.

Backing slowly into a jackknife without his trailer brakes, Colter had no sense of where the trailer was going, even with it clearly vis-ible in the rearview mirror. It was as if the trailer were already dis-connected, no longer that familiar extension of his arms and legs and brain, and it made him uncomfortable having to snug the trailer in so tight against the wall of the station. He felt naked and more than a little incompetent with a disabled rig and the cold, hard eyes of the law watching his every move. Once the trailer was in position, he released the breakaway valve with a great rush of escaping air, doused the running lights, and carefully stowed his hat on the bunk behind the driver's seat, out of harm's way. When Colter climbed down out of the cab again he left Leon asleep on the shotgun side. The wind whipped horizontally across the barren drive, churning the snow up in his face as he set the wooden chocks firmly against the rear duals. Then came the hard part.

First he had to hand crank the landing gear down until that almost imperceptible moment when the front weight of the trailer lifted, and he could stow the crank handle again. No problem, that. But pulling the fifth wheel kingpin lock was a pain in the ass under the best of conditions. Metal became harder to work with the colder it got. It was damn cold now, and with the metal this cold the grease coating on the fifth wheel had stiffened to a nearly solid state. Absolutely certain that the nightwatchman, the boy in the station, and now everybody in the diner were all watching, he tugged on the pin a time or two with no results. Stuck fast in the frozen grease. He pulled again, harder this time, huffing and puffing, thinking as he yanked that he really should go in for a checkup sometime soon. Nothing. Then, out of sheer desperation, Colter cocked one knee against the truck frame and, throwing his weight into the pull, finally yanked the pin out and into its locked position, rolling ass over teacup onto the drive in the process. Recovering as nonchalantly as possible, not wanting to make any eye contact at all with his audience, he bowed stiffly from the waist to adjust his lower back, then climbed carefully up into the narrow space between the trailer and the back of the tractor cab. After disconnecting the glad-hands, the umbilical air line connectors, and electrical pigtail that gave life to all the trailer systems, he stowed them tightly into their waiting loops of bungee cord, climbed coolly around and into the open door of the cab without touching the ground again, and inched the tractor slowly away from the dead hulk of the trailer, thinking to top off the driver-side fuel tank when he didn't have an audience.

With the roar of the diesel engine and the vibrations of the massive pistons slightly rocking the cab, Colter felt instantly the pull of the road, that magnetic, nearly overpowering urge to move, to head out onto the highway again toward somewhere. Anywhere but here. Like good dope, he loved the road, hooked on the act of moving, and hated it all at the same time. Nothing like those two fountains of profound insight and advice, either, to keep a guy on the straight and narrow. Wife says quit driving altogether and come home. Soon, though. Not right now. Hints at consequences, inconvenience. Dispatch says stay. Now. Or there'll be consequences. So now, with nothing to do but wait out the storm and slow, slow repairs, Colter supposed he'd have to settle for a reluctant tour, see how the little burg might have fared in the last thirty years. And on the way, maybe suffer a brief graveside chat with Dad.

A quick, comforting glance in the rearview mirror suggested the oversized nightwatchman might have finally found something more interesting to watch. He was nowhere to be seen.

Chapter Eleven

The little cemetery lay beneath a hillside grove of dark cedars just off the State Road 33 spur that ran between I-40 and the town proper. Colter knew he'd put this one off too long, tired or not. Despite Marilyn's compulsion for control, he knew she was right. He hated the thought of going to the graveside empty-handed, but on the other hand, he couldn't imagine bringing his father, alive or dead, a flower.

In clear weather the hillside commanded a pleasant view of the surrounding countryside. Colter could remember a picturesque bend in the river visible from the highest point, next to the little clapboard Mennonite church. Now, in the blinding snow, he could hardly see the turnoff, the cedars suddenly appearing as ghostly shadows across the hillside. He followed the tracks from another vehicle through the snow leading up the drive onto the hill. Toward the top the faint shape of the little white church with its distinctive square bell tower and sturdy cross slowly emerged from the white gauze of snow on the right, while to his left the dark, irregular shape of the cedars loomed heavily above the crowded field of snowcapped stones. Off in the far corner Colter could just make out the indistinct yellow scorpion-shaped backhoe. It stood next to the rear fence beside a huge mound of surplus soil, the reddish hue of the soil barely showing through the drifted, windblown snow.

Looking out beneath the cedars, beyond the rows of leaning stones toward the boundary fence, Colter knew immediately that he was alone in his early morning pilgrimage. Whoever had come earlier and broken a track up the snowy driveway had left again, leaving behind a double path of footprints leading straight out across the grove and back. Such directness suggested a practiced, ritual visit, and Colter realized with a twinge of guilt that he had no idea where his father lay buried, that his own wandering tracks through the snow would tell a tale of prodigal indifference, neglect.

Near the entrance gate stood a convenient fifty-five-gallon trash drum painted a cheerful pink and full to overflowing with all shapes and colors and sizes of faded plastic flowers. The flowers, recently harvested from the rows of graves in preparation for the new crop of Easter lilies, had spilled over onto the ground in somber profusion, their stems and faded blossoms showing through the shroud of snow like a faint memory of summer. He parked the idling truck in an open area near the flower barrel, and conscious suddenly of the intrusive noise of the diesel in the silent grove, shut off the engine for the first time in twenty-four hours. Into the silence Leon yawned and stretched, hesitating before making his slow and painful descent off the seat so that Colter could lift him down out of the cab. Once on the ground, he seemed to look uncomprehendingly at the snow for a moment, then, with a deliberate wag of his tail, set off for the nearest headstone.

Bewildered at the rows of silent, leaning stones in the old cemetery, Colter noticed again the pink barrel full of plastic flowers and in an instant knew exactly the token offering he would leave. In the drought-plagued fifties his father had cajoled most of the downtown merchants into opting for two blocks of utterly tasteless aluminum false fronts to hide the old, turn-of-the-century red brick facades along Main and Broadway. It was all done in the name of progress and community pride, and Colter could remember his father and grandfather arguing about it over Sunday dinner. What more fitting memorial for such a man than a plastic flower? Dusting the snow from a particularly gaudy stalk of faded purple iris with its wand of green plastic leaf, Colter sensed he might not yet be in the proper frame of mind for this visit.

The wind had slacked off, and the sky responded by dumping a load of flakes the size of nickels, so that the hilltop took on the aspects of an island, isolate and remote from the rest of the landscape. The falling snow softened the rigid outlines of the rectangular little church and bell tower, reduced all but the nearest cedars to gray shadows, and magically erased the countryside round about the hill. Alone in the silence, while Leon cast about with the restrained enthusiasm of an old dog on the hunt again, Colter began to make his way among the rows of stones, alert for a low mound of snow-covered earth without a headstone. The mound, after only a few months now, would not have the height of a fresh grave. Nevertheless, it should, by his calculations, still be recognizable as a mound, and it came to him suddenly as he paused beneath the sheltering boughs of cedar that he was thinking in pretty casual terms of his father's final resting place, the dark house of his bones. His father's remains. All that remained of his father. Jesus. He wondered for a fleeting second at the morbid state of the decomposing body, his mind moving quickly to the quality of the casket, and then on to the nature of the graveside service Marilyn's money had provided in his absence. What might a passing stranger, driving by on the highway, have thought of the grand procession as it approached the cemetery hill, car lights ablaze on such a fine and sunny afternoon as he was now imagining? He wondered what hymns might have been sung.

Given the gulf of their differences, he also realized with an unexpected welling of anger that his father was actually gone, that he would not see him again. He and his father suffered from truly irreconcilable differences now, and Colter had no clue how to go about making peace with a dead man. It made him angry all over again, as if his father had no business dying just yet. He felt the same way about having somehow missed the war in Vietnam while the best of his generation was busy dying in the jungle. His only war, and no way to go back and do it over again. In a brief flash of insight, Colter realized that he had probably kept the little pistol close at hand all these years just for a second chance to fight. Despite his half century of experience in losing things, it was still very difficult for Colter to accept that when some things went away, they really went away. He tried to hold on to the strange, sort of silly notion that his father was somehow still around, accepting the old man's subtle presence because in the end Colter simply couldn't imagine where he might have gone.

In thirty years away, he found, too, that he really had forgotten the location of the family plot. Not that it was a plot, really. More a line of modest graves, the stones shrinking over time in relation to the rising cost of fine marble and the labor to carve it. At the death of his little sister two years before his own birth, the notion of monument in the Tyree family had apparently been reduced to gray cement. He remembered her short little life bracketed by dates on a simple bronze plaque, set, he supposed, while the poured concrete headstone hardened inside its confining wooden form. This had happened in the early years of his parents' marriage, before prosperity began attaching itself again for one last, glorious ride to his father's generation. He remembered a time, too, another winter day standing in this same cemetery, attending the burial of a much-beloved great uncle. Funny that he could remember the day so clearly, could recall the sinister coffin shape of a cloud overhead, the cold, fierce wind where they stood between the trees. But for the life of him, he couldn't remember exactly where they stood. In wandering slowly up and down the rows of headstones Colter tried to think of what he might say when he found the right mound, but he could no more come up with anything profound than he could find his way through the maze of stones. Maybe Oliver was right. Maybe absolution was all he sought. Maybe forgiveness for having gone off and pissed away his life. For not having fought in his own war. Perhaps forgiveness for never having come back home, for not having followed in the proverbial footsteps. For his determined irresponsibility, his needfulness, thinking now of the money his father had sent over the years, each charitable donation another red mark in the failure column of their own private ledger. For never having been the kind of son he knew his father always wanted. Colter had seen his father in the years since he had left, but only on Colter's own terms and his own turf. Now lonely much of the time on the road, essentially childless in light of his own grown-up and indifferent offspring, hardly even married anymore for chrissake, who, he wondered, might remain at the end to mourn Colter Wayne Tyree.

The morning was wearing on. Colter was beat after the all-night drive from Albuquerque, and now his feet felt wet and cold in the thin Nikes. Leon soon tired of the snow and the cold and occasionally shot a backward glance over his shoulder, clearly eager to end this foolishness. So with one parting, futile glance out across cemetery, Colter turned back, knowing that any further discussions with his father would just have to wait. Leon pranced ahead like a barn-broke horse, no doubt ready for his morning can of Strongheart and a short nap on the shotgun seat.

Before cranking up the diesel and backing the tractor around to head out the drive again, Colter tossed the long-stemmed iris. Missing the barrel, he watched his intended graveside offering sail beyond the scatter of plastic onto the snow-covered ground, its bright colors and defined shape leaping out from the shapeless white world like a green and purple flame.

Chapter Twelve

Seeing Oliver again, and now the deserted cemetery, had loosed a flood of memory. For old time's sake, and as long as he was still on this side of the river and had a little time and an ounce of energy left, Colter decided to run down past the park and football stadium and take a quick look at Oliver's old house. He should have asked, pinned it down, but Oliver's comment about the outhouse suggested someone still lived there. The place had always been a communal house where poor, often alcoholic, and always needy relatives came and went like waves. If the house still stood, anybody might be living there. Auntie Myrtle was already old when Colter was a boy forty years ago; he couldn't imagine her alive today.

Back on the highway, winding the lighter-than-air diesel cab through its gears, he watched for the nightwatchman's black pickup truck but the snow-packed road was clear of traffic all the way back to the turnoff.

The first thing wrong was that the football stadium was gone. Colter hadn't even started school when they tore down the old rodeo grounds with its arena and loading chutes to put in the new football bleachers. His dad had taken him to watch one afternoon after work, and he remembered weathered planks from the ancient corral sticking out of the top of a departing dump truck. He recalled how crisp and white the new bleachers looked and how their whiteness matched the chalk lines on the new Bermuda sod. The home team bleachers and concession stand had backed up to the announcer's box, a wooden contraption stuck up on four telephone poles that later doubled as a civil air patrol spotting tower. Nothing would ever dull the high school memory of those cold Friday nights in November, the field an emerald green under the glare of floodlights, he and Rae Lynn wrapped together in a wool blanket while they cheered on the hometown heroes. A simpler time, long since gone. He wondered with more than idle curiosity if she had actually stuck it out, later, with the quarterback.

Now even the bleachers were gone. All that remained was a ragged stand of winterkilled fireweed taking over the old Bermuda turf. The open area of the football field was still surrounded by huge cottonwood trees, though, which he suddenly began to look upon as old and loyal friends, and the dirt lane still wandered dependably off on the far side toward Buck's pasture and the Indian house.

He could almost see, through the years and the falling snow, the three little boys, two Indians and one skinny white kid, leaping from that sagging porch, fast on their way to some amazing adventure in the nearby woods of Buck's pasture. He could remember the three of them hiking up the meandering creek on long summer Saturdays all the way to the spring seep where the creek began beside the old cellar that sat back in the cattails below his grandfather's abandoned farmhouse. He could remember the raucous calls of crows piercing the summer mornings, suddenly realizing that his memories were nearly always of summer.

Colter even remembered the two-holer Oliver had mentioned, with the wasp nest that always got rebuilt above the doorway no matter how many times Auntie Myrtle would knock it down with a broom handle, and just inside the door, the broken sack of quicklime with its carved wooden scoop. He remembered how you rolled a sheet of newspaper from the stack beside the seat, lit it with a match from the ready box of wooden kitchen matches, and swept the burning torch around beneath the edge of the hole to scorch the black widows. Auntie Myrtle had taught him to do it long before anyone in his own household would have dreamed of trusting little Cole Tyree, the banker's son, with a match. Never mind that Colter could not imagine why anyone would ever need an outhouse with two seats.

Looking back, he knew his good times must have been bought and paid for: Auntie Myrtle, a paid housekeeper and babysitter, and her two nephews her captive helpers. And when they came into town on cleaning days it had never occurred to Colter how much they probably ached to play with his roomful of toys, to have played a Gene Autry record, *Red River Valley* maybe, on his little green record player. Oliver had mentioned the peanut butter sandwiches, the sliced apples from his grandmother, but they were always picnics, it was always summer, and they always ate at the redwood table set under the spreading elm outside the back door. Like hired help, which they were. What might it have meant to have had a peanut butter sandwich on a clean, white plate in a bright, sunny kitchen, and to have had his grandmother hover over them, filling up their milk glasses before they had time to empty them, or maybe just get to use the inside toilet once.

Closer to the house now, Colter left the engine idling, set the parking brake, and climbed down out of the truck cab, leaving Leon asleep on the seat. As he walked up the nearly overgrown two-track road where few vehicles obviously went anymore, Colter could feel the past pressing in. There were clear footprints through the snow this morning, a set toward the house and a return set that detoured to the edge of the woods and the telltale yellow snow of a winter sunflower. Looking up the hill toward the old house, Colter could almost imagine the old woman rocking away on the dilapidated porch.

The house was far smaller, grayer looking than he remembered. It was set into the side of a hill beside a little spring seep at the head of a wooded draw, and Colter immediately noticed the way the faded yellow brick-patterned tar paper hung in tatters off the near corner, leaving the wood siding exposed. The roof had been patched so many times and with so many different colored scraps and shapes of tar paper that it looked like the roof of many colors, and in the lower corner toward the front Colter could see the spaced decking boards laid bare, as if the skin had been peeled back, revealing gray bone.

The wind was up again, rushing overhead through the bare branches with a constant moan. This last spring storm, falling just at Easter, threatened to lock the world into perpetual winter dusk. Snow had drifted along the dirt road, piling up on the lee side of the trees and behind the scrub sumac, and looking off into the woods, all Colter could see was a tangled web of dark trees, black and then gray and then gone as the falling snow shut out everything beyond.

The road curved beneath the elms, their branches touching overhead, and from childhood he remembered this lane as dark, foreboding, with the Indian house always flooded with sunlight at the end. Now, with the trees bare overhead, the sky a flat gray overcast with the snow falling as if there were no sky at all, there was just the familiar red dirt where the wind had swept the road open in places, the blowing snow and the dark skeleton trees, bare black bones linking heaven and earth, and beyond it all, the dark outline of the house emerging from the white sky.

For a fleeting second, looking at the old house from the lane, Colter could sense again in his aching bones the weight of his own life's journey. How could this place from his childhood, a place of such vivid beginnings, such dreaming, now look so utterly abandoned, faded to this grayness? He listened to the incessant moaning of the wind through the top branches of the bare trees, held his breath while it whistled around the eaves.

There were always dogs. They would come out from beneath the porch on a summer morning barking fiercely and wagging their tails at the same time. He remembered at least two or three nondescript hounds and one blind old collie. He always felt bad for the collie. Her hair was always matted with thorns, and he knew that beneath that matted coat she was probably starving, last to feed among the pack.

Now there was no sound save the wind and the banging of a loose board somewhere on the back side of the house. Occasionally a patch of roof paper would lift silently then lay flat again as the gust passed. Then he noticed the footprints again around the old hand pump in the yard, and a soft, yellow glow coming from behind the right side window next to the front door, and Colter felt another quickening in his chest. The kitchen, he remembered, lay just inside the front door to the right, just off the central hall, and he knew in an instant the old woman was still alive. He knew she would be inside, and his first impulse was to turn and run, go back to the truck, drive away, and never see this place again.

Instead, he approached the porch from the path coming up the lane, half expecting the dogs even though they had certainly been dead now these many years. Auntie Myrtle would have to be in her nineties. Maybe even a hundred. Colter couldn't imagine how anyone could be living out here, much less an old, old woman. But when he thought of it, where else would she go? Who did she ever have but a worthless niece who ran off with that poor white trash then died early and left her to raise Oliver and Johnny? With Johnny gone for good and Oliver busy entertaining his waitress friend in a teepee or an Airstream, where would she go? If she was really inside, she had certainly outlived most of her generation as well as the next. Oliver probably brought her things from the store and looked in on her from time to time. Maybe even dealt with the tribal human services people on her behalf. Her crazy and dutiful nephew. Colter realized that Auntie Myrtle was probably the only reason Oliver had come back to Fairview at all.

Colter approached the house warily through the falling snow, thinking surely he was imagining things. No house that looked like this one could be inhabited. He remembered a rare overnight childhood visit here, refuge, no doubt, from some family emergency. The boys slept in the little lean-to bedroom long since gone to firewood off the back hall. He remembered the coming of daylight through the wood siding where the boards, drying and shrinking in the fierce sunlight of summer, had pulled apart in places. In the morning the cracks between the boards made rays of sunlight where the dust motes danced. How the snowflakes would dance through them now, he thought.

The cold porch boards creaked with his weight. He paused at the threshold as if waiting for a sign, but hearing nothing, silently pushed aside the sagging screen door and opened the front door. To the right, just inside the kitchen, on the otherwise bare wooden table, sat an unopened brown sack of groceries in the pale light from a bare overhead light bulb. There was no sink. Funny to remember just now, but there never had been one. A water bucket and aluminum dipper still stood next to a white tin dishpan on the plywood countertop. The cupboards, doorless just as Colter remembered them, were empty save a few red and white Campbell's soup cans and a blue and yellow box of Kraft macaroni and cheese. The floors were swept clean; the broom and dustpan leaned in a far corner beside an oversize, baited rattrap.

Next to the wood cookstove and near enough to reach the neat stack of stove wood, the old woman lay wrapped like a mummy in an army surplus sleeping bag on a mattress of disassembled cardboard boxes spread atop a folding army cot. It was as if someone had gathered the life from the reaches of the dark house and concentrated it here, into the heartspace, like a single candle flame. The room held a faint warmth from cooling embers deep inside the cookstove, but beyond the hall door Colter could sense empty rooms, could imagine faded wallpaper peeling off the old lath-and-plaster walls in long, thin tatters, the plaster falling away to reveal the bones of lath beneath. The life had mostly gone out of the house. Only her shrunken face and tumbled flow of silver, unbraided hair peeked out the top of the green mummy bag, and it wasn't until she whistled a little snore that Colter was even sure she was alive.

She awoke calmly, without any fear in her eyes at all, as if whatever might be done to her had already been done long ago. Nothing would surprise her now, nothing could touch her. It was as if she were already beyond the living, out farther near the edge than even Colter dared to go, and so there was a calmness, a peace in her voice as she spoke his name. "Cole Tyree," she said simply.

"Yes, Auntie Myrtle," he said. "Yes."

"I knew one day you'd come home."

"Auntie, I haven't seen you in almost forty years. How can you know me? How can you possibly know me?" How could you ever have known me, he thought.

"I see good," she smiled. "I know what I see, and I see good."

He just looked down at her. She made no move to stir, to get off the cot. She simply looked at him across the years and smiled her toothless smile.

"And how did you know I'd come, Auntie?" he asked, smiling at the thought of Oliver bringing in the groceries.

"I see even better in my dreams," she said, smiling back, just the hint of a twinkle in her clouded eyes. "Coyote told me you'd come."

Her skin was sunken against the bones of her skull, drawn back as if from the weight of that shock of strong, silver hair that lay about her head. He had never seen an old person with such hair. The sight of it reminded him of a story from Ripley's Believe It or Not, about some of the bodies in the catacombs beneath Paris, their hair growing long and red, feeding on the substance of the body long after death. He wanted to pull back the folds of the sleeping bag to look at her hands, half expecting to see curled fingernails a foot long.

"I am not dead," she said as if reading his mind. "Not yet."

"You are so old, Auntie Myrtle."

"I think maybe one hundred, I don't know. We didn't keep to those things. I feel one hundred. Some days, maybe more." She smiled again with her gums.

It was awkward, and tiring, to stand while she lay on the cot, but he did not want to pull out the only kitchen chair from the table for fear she would vanish like smoke from the room. "Why are you living out here all alone, Auntie?" he asked.

"Because I'm one hundred years old," she said, "and I can do what I want."

"You should be in town," he said, "in a warm house with clean sheets." The thought of a warm room with clean white sheets, after the long drive, all he had been through, was almost too much to bear.

"I have to have the fresh air," she said.

Colter said nothing.

"I could not breathe in a house in town, all closed up so you can't feel the air move. That town air is dead," she said. "Where's Johnny?"

Here we go, Colter thought. Fairview Oklahoma's version of a homeless crazy. A street person finally too old to push a shopping cart around. "Johnny's gone," he said softly. "He's been gone a long time now, Auntie."

"Oh. I forget. They think he is eating dogs," she said. "They say he's gone crazy, walking around backward like a dog soldier, and they say he eats dogs, like in old times, the time of my mother, but it's not so."

"Who, Auntie? Who is crazy?" Who is crazy here, he thought. Just exactly who?

"Oliver," she said. "Gut-eater, that big sheriff calls him. You have to help. I wonder where's Johnny got off to since the war?"

Had them mixed up, thinking they went off to war together. All the time she smiled at him, genuinely glad to see him, her face full of recognition, and yet she made no more sense than a talking crow.

"His life is going away. He is lost. I should be walking away on the star path, but it's Oliver going away. He's put up with me all these years, but now he's going away. They say he eats the dogs, ahh," she said with a sudden gesture of her hand inside the sleeping bag, as if to say stupid, how stupid of them to say that. Colter didn't know whether to sit down politely on the single chair or stand very still and let all this wash over him. He stood. The straining of the old house to hold against the wind, the occasional snowflake drifting in from the open door into the hall, the air, cold and dry against his face, all this was real. But how could this old woman, this shriveled ghost from his distant past, his childhood, be real? She was like a phantom, a wisp of air, her voice as cracked as her face, the lines going in deeper than her skin so that it cracked her very voice in half. Craziness. How could she talk of eating dogs? Like in old times, she had said, in her mother's time.

"Is there anything I can do for you, Auntie?"

"Help him. You never got on after you grew up. Two can be strong. So strong, you know."

"How can I help? I'm a truck driver, Auntie. I don't even live here anymore. My truck broke down out on the highway so I'm here to see you for a minute. But I'm not really here. Not really."

She brought out a brown and shrunken hand from beneath the quilted sleeping bag for him to accept. There were no long, curving fingernails. Just the frail hand of an old, old woman, the hand strangely warm, soft to the touch like suede.

"You're here," she said. "Help him."

"Help him how?"

"Find Johnny."

Colter smiled. "Johnny's gone," he said again, as gently as he could.

"You find Johnny," the old woman said, her face animated now, with just a hint of fear. The peace was gone like smoke, and in its place, urgency. "He helps me, and he helps that nice white woman, too, and the rest of them, and now you have to help him. I can't help him anymore."

"Where do I find him, Auntie?" He was thinking maybe he needed to go back into town and call the authorities. He couldn't leave this old woman, raving in her madness, out here alone to die of exposure, starvation, but he couldn't imagine trying to talk to the nightwatchman about the problem, either.

"Two are strong," she said again. "I'm glad to see you. You have to go away now. I have to go on and sleep some more." She moved slightly in the sleeping bag, gently withdrawing her hand and turning her head toward the wall, and she didn't stir again.

By the time Colter unpacked the groceries, a can of commodity coffee with a white label that simply said "Coffee," a brick of welfare cheese, a can each of Carnation evaporated milk and Campbell's tomato soup, and left, the snow was slacking off. The wind still whistled through the bare branches of the trees along the creek and howled around the eaves of the old house, whipping flakes into the air, but the snow had stopped falling from the sky, a temporary lull in the storm. At least that. The storm had rolled in out of the northwest, and now he could imagine beyond the wall of trees, out near the lost horizon toward Woodward, far away on the plains even beyond the curve of the earth, a thin little line of blue off at the edge of the world showing beneath the blanket of gray. For a moment he could hear his father's voice saying, "Big as a Dutchman's pants," Clinton Tyree explaining to his son that anytime you could see a patch of blue sky as big as a Dutchman's pants, the sky would surely clear. The single gem of wisdom had stuck, leaving Colter to forever measure the sky on a cloudy day. The air stung sharply on his face as he stepped out of the shelter of the porch and headed back into the wind toward the truck, but where before there had been only the flat and gray of a featureless sky, now there was at least a shape of light and shadow to the underside of the clouds. Maybe the worst of the snow is over, he thought. A few small drifts had piled up where the wind had whipped the blowing snow into the woods. The creek bottom lay white and still except where the dark water showed through, and now, if the wind would blow itself out like the kid at the station had said, he might actually be able to hit the road again. Catch a quick flight out of Okie City for the weekend, maybe. Surprise Marilyn with a dozen red roses. Tired to the bone, Colter knew he could never do it, never mind the money. And if he somehow managed to make it to the city, get a flight out, what then? Crash all weekend with the sleep of the dead. Marilyn would certainly find that stimulating. And what might he find, coming home unexpected like that. Rule of the road was, you always called ahead. He'd never thought much about it until now.

Once back at the truck, it was time for Leon to pee again, and Colter welcomed the diversion. Someone was going to have to deal responsibly with Auntie Myrtle, and it was going to be Oliver. He made up his mind to speak to him about it before he left town. Maybe talk about other things, too. The river, maybe. Colter had been gone a long time.

Coming up out of the old park, the diesel engine throbbing again into the silent woods, Colter recalled the new bridge off the frontage road. Driving back and forth along the interstate, he'd watched them building it with some interest. But as long as he was here, he wanted first to see the old things, to see if there was anything left at all the way he remembered it.

He was nearly a mile down the narrow little spur, coming up on the old 1920s Erector Set bridge over the North Canadian and already thinking of those clean white sheets on the other side, when a quick glance at the rearview mirror revealed a flashing red light. Sure enough, the nightwatchman's macho little truck was crawling silently along behind, matching exactly Colter's same slow, cautious creep across the snow. He thought it odd to see the light flashing so furiously in near silence, the only sounds a little whistling from the heater and his rear dual chains making a soft crunching on the snowpack.

Chapter Thirteen

Colter feathered the brake pedal, bringing the tractor to a smooth, quiet stop on the last approach to the bridge. Below and immediately in front of the truck lay the overgrown, tangled, snowy banks of the North Canadian, the river a swollen flood of muddy water as dark and red as the River Styx. Through the trees and the once again falling snow, beyond the far bank, he could barely see a scatter of white houses, all but invisible save their darkened windows, and the curving surface of the old road into town. Those clean sheets might as well be on the far side of the moon, he thought.

Colter had set the parking brake and was about to open the cab door when he heard the thin, amplified voice of the nightwatchman twanging over a megaphone.

"Please step out of the cab slowly," the voice was saying into the empty woods around them, "keeping your hands visible at all times."

Colter could feel his heart beating again, flooding his body with adrenaline. He could even feel his pulse in the little vein at the side of his temple. Jesus, what the fuck now, he thought, the fatigue suddenly gone. The whole thing seemed right out of a B movie. Isolated spot, overweight, small-town, southern sheriff with a chip on his shoulder.

He nearly palmed the little .32, then immediately thought better of it. This can't be happening. Not right here in broad daylight, for chrissake. Instead, he pushed the gun out of sight down into the crack between the bucket seat and backrest and opened the door. With both hands visible on the doorframe, just as instructed, he stepped down onto the running board then onto the snowpack again, facing the little black truck, the red light flashing silently on the falling snow, the woods around.

"Would you mind telling me what this is all about, officer?" he said, trying to move out of earshot of the open cab door to avoid waking Leon. Keeping his hands down but visible and at his sides he spoke in an even tone, but over his voice he could hear Leon stirring, yawning. ChristJesus. All he needed now was for that fucking dog to get his second wind. The nightwatchman still hadn't stepped out of his pickup, but Colter could see him clearly through the windshield holding the mike for the roof-mounted megaphone.

"You can't drive across on that old bridge," the twangy voice came out. "Won't hold your weight. We route trucks in over the new one now. Guess you wouldn't know that, being from out of town and all."

There was just the slightest hint of a test in it. Nothing definite, not really an outright challenge. Not enough to be sure. He thought about the kid at the station, but then the nightwatchman was a newcomer, too. Oliver said so. Then he remembered the farm and the part about this idiot digging up graves, and Colter knew the name Tyree would mean something after all.

"Thanks, officer," he said. "I appreciate your letting me know." He had stopped his advance and was standing alone in the middle of the road, the snow falling lightly all around him again with a sudden lull in the wind. He really didn't want to approach the nightwatchman's truck and had started to turn away when the megaphone voice called out, "Hold on just a minute, son."

There was that "son" crap again.

He stopped in midturn, knowing immediately he had flunked, and looked back through the windshield where the nightwatchman was holding the megaphone mike in one hand and talking into another, a CB mike, his huge hands nearly swallowing both black microphones like little tiny black boxes. Then the officer replaced the megaphone mike back onto its dashboard hook and opened the pickup door. Still holding the CB, he leaned around the windshield.

"When we met earlier, I don't recall where you said you were from. Could you perhaps enlighten me? Matter of fact, your name has even slipped my mind. Just for my records, you know." That singsong voice again, soft and sweet as arsenic molasses, while the nightwatchman replaced the CB mike and began to unfold himself from the confines of his pickup.

Shit, Colter's thinking, keep the voice incredulous, not defiant. Always remember that the last thing we need is another moving violation on our slightly tarnished record. He could hear Leon yawning, for chrissake, in the cab.

"I'm sorry, officer," Colter said. "Are you citing me for something? If there was a sign, I missed it."

"No, no. I'm not going to arrest you. Nothing like that," he said, turning his incredible bulk out of the pickup toward the middle of the road. "I just don't want anyone hurt on my watch. But I do keep records. Who I see roundabout town. That sort of thing. There is a sign, by the way."

"No problem, officer." Colter's thinking, enough of this bullshit. "Name's Tyree. Colter Wayne Tyree. I live in New Mexico. But you probably know that already."

The nightwatchman smiled. "Actually I do, son. Ran the door codes off the cab back to your dispatch." He brushed the hair off his forehead, and with it a light gathering of snowflakes. "But I appreciate your candor. I really do. Are you planning to stay around town long? I mean after your truck is repaired."

"Now why would I do that?" Thinking that now, of course, with dispatch knowing damn well where he was, a law enforcement inquiry might just prompt a peek into his personnel file. Two plus two equals convenient Easter weekend off in old hometown.

"Just a thought. Seemed like something familiar about your name. Seemed like a name I've heard before. Maybe you have family here?"

"Had."

"Tyree . . . Tyree . . . wasn't there a Tyree owned a bank hereabouts?

Died not too long ago? I'm a newcomer to these parts, but seems like I remember mention of a Tyree. And another fella named Tyree was a farmer here, too, if I'm not mistaken. Of course, that would have been long before I arrived."

"The same." Colter sure wasn't going to make this any easier, but in the back of his mind he knew they were both guilty of some very bad acting.

The nightwatchman didn't say anything, nor did he seem to be pretending anymore that he was trying to figure anything out. He just looked at Colter with a blank stare. Neither smile nor frown. Just a waiting stare.

"Officer, I don't know what the problem is," Colter finally said, knowing full well the first one to talk had just lost. He tried shifting his weight into a more relaxed stance. "I can tell you I have a load waiting in Oklahoma City, which I am supposed to deliver to St. Louis by no later than Monday night. Not that it's really any of your business, but as you noticed over at the diner, the truck was damaged out on the highway, and I pulled off at the first exit. As I'm sure you also know by now, I grew up here, and although I left a long time ago, I am now, by default, a local property owner, or at least it appeared so when I got the attorney's bill for probate. I had no intention of ever coming back here. From what I've seen so far, the old home place won't bring much at public auction, but whatever it will bring, I certainly have no intention of dealing with it now. I don't believe in coincidence any more than you do, but I can tell you that's what this is. I'm stuck here until the rig is fixed and my plan is to leave as soon as that's accomplished, but it's a free country, and I really don't care if you believe I'm leaving or not." Thinking he's on a roll now, "This is my hometown, and I'll stay as long as I want. I have violated no laws that I'm aware of, nor do I intend to violate any, but I can assure you I won't be run out of town by a municipal nightwatchman who's seen too many grade-B westerns. I thank you for warning me about the bridge. I have been gone a long time, it seems. Maybe too long." Pushing the envelope now, adrenaline up, feet wide apart, Colter could feel the backward lift of his shoulders squaring. "Now is there anything else I can do for you? Anything at all? Do we need to discuss anything else about the old Tyree place? Do you maybe want to buy it for the mineral rights? I understand there may be some unauthorized mining operations underway."

The nightwatchman was smiling again, his massive head looking like a horse's head carved from pink granite.

"I detect a slight belligerence in your voice, son. Maybe we just got off on the wrong foot somehow. For that I apologize." He began to unbutton the front of his long, black overcoat casually, as if he were merely too warm. "Probably had to do with the dog. I didn't expect to find a dog in the place where I eat breakfast. Not a live one at any rate. Then, too, people don't like me for my size, but I can live with that, too. But I have sworn an oath to look out for the interests of the people of this little . . . municipality . . . as you referred to it." He pulled the coat back off his right side, revealing a holstered .45 semiautomatic, the unsnapped holster hanging off what had to be two wide leather belts stitched together and buckled around the middle of his overalls. He made no move to draw it, but the gesture made it clear the weapon was available. "I'm not going to arrest you, son, but I will want to see the registration and carry permit for that little popgun you left in the seat when you went into the diner this morning. I assume you had the good sense to leave it in the cab when you stepped out a moment ago."

It was a strain for Colter to keep his mouth from falling open. This asshole had checked out the rig before he even came into the diner. Of course there was no paperwork at all for the .32. Colter had bought it clean, out the back door of an Amarillo pawnshop, the year he started driving. Without a gun you ran the risk of accidentally stumbling over the edge unprepared. With the gun, you lived on the edge. Life was simple. The gun was the edge. Company policy strictly forbade drivers carrying a weapon. Insurance problems, they said. Colter could never understand their position, thinking instead of the .32 as insurance. But a moving violation was beginning to look pretty good next to an out-of-state weapons charge. Jesus. Here he stood, one foot on a banana peel, the other already over the cliff. Again.

By the time they managed to sort it out without anyone getting shot, Colter had surrendered the weapon temporarily until his rig was repaired and he was ready to leave. The deal was, he could pick up the

.32 on his way out of town as long as the rig was intact, the trailer road-worthy. The officer would have the gun with him for safekeeping, with no other city personnel even involved. In return for the officer kindly agreeing not to further raise the issue of a weapons charge with district court in Watonga, the county seat, Colter would agree to leave as soon as the rig was ready, and would agree not to bring an unregistered weapon back into Fairview under any circumstances. It was, after all, against the law, and they both agreed that it was in Colter's best interest to remain a law-abiding citizen. As to the alleged mining operations on the old Tyree home place, the officer knew nothing at all. It was out of his jurisdiction, being outside the town limits and all, but he would certainly look into it, time permitting, of course.

As soon as the little pickup began to back up the deserted spur road toward the interstate, Colter immediately coaxed Leon out to pee, but he didn't really begin breathing normally again until the nightwatchman disappeared from sight around the first curve in the frontage road.

No way was Colter going anywhere now. No way in hell. Marilyn's flowers could wait. As far as Colter was concerned, the goddamn beef could even wait. This asshole cop had all but blackmailed him to leave, and Colter decided then and there to play it out. The farm, as he thought about it, was his only birthright. Looking around at all the local prosperity, it probably didn't amount to much. He figured it was worth something, though, and he might as well look into it while he was here.

But the incident with the gun, like the proverbial last straw, had finally done him in. That little situation was too close to getting out of hand. Hassled or not, the next stop was going to be the registration desk of the old hotel, downtown Fairview, Oklahoma, before his judgment abandoned him for good. He was actually glad he hadn't climbed down out of the truck with the little .32 stuffed in his back pocket. A nuisance not to have it, but at least no one was dead now. Jesus, talk about a cowboy. Come Monday he would look into filing some sort of complaint. He was sure somebody in this town would remember his family favorably. Somebody with a little clout. Main thing was, Colter badly needed a good night's sleep, and in something slightly larger than a tin can.

Thinking a room with a view would be nice. And clean white sheets.

Chapter Fourteen

Because of the damn nightwatchman, Colter ended up coming into town from the south, across the newer wide-span bridge, a belated monument to his father's dwindling civic influence in the early '90s.

He knew from a stack of unanswered letters the bridge had been the result of an intense lobbying effort, successful in the end because the town probably needed it, allowing a painless payback for years of loyal political support from the district's retiring state representative. He also knew the south approach off the frontage road included a granite monument and bronze plaque commemorating his father and the representative, "without whose tireless dedication this much-needed bridge would never have been possible, blah, blah, blah . . ." Colter remembered some of the wording from trying to decipher the old man's failing penmanship. He also remembered that the plaque noted, in sanitized terms, the reason for the town: a low-water cavalry crossing on the North Canadian. Truth be known, camp followers had probably established the town around a convenient cantonment for mounted troops making the long ride from Ft. Reno to Ft. Supply during a decade of Indian unrest following the Civil War. Cantonment, he thought. Now there was a hundred-dollar word he would never have known if he hadn't grown up here.

The bridge brought him in on a stretch of new road that cut through a remembered wheat field and dumped him suddenly onto the south end of Broadway, just down the street from his childhood home. That distinctive cedar shelterbelt, planted he thought around 1912 as a row of coffee-can seedlings along the side of the house by his grandfather, still stood out like a flotilla of dark-sailed ships. The cedars all leaned to the north from the hot, dry south wind that blew straight up from Texas during the summer growing season.

First thing he noticed, all the lower branches had been sawed off. The tangle of perfect climbing branches were gone now, as were the giant spreading elms in the front yard that had shaded the two-story white clapboard house. Without the stately elms in front, and with the cedars trimmed up to stand on silly stilts along the south side, the house looked much smaller, bare and exposed even, vulnerable somehow in this harsh prairie storm. The last house out on the south side of town, it had been his grandparents' home when they first moved in from the farm. Colter and his parents had moved into it following his grandmother's death back in the fifties. His own first house, the little two-room bungalow Colter's father had built on the vacant lot next door, was gone entirely. In its place sat a squat, brown singlewide moved onto the lot fairly recently, judging from the trench for a new sewer line that ran like a long, open grave from the street.

Just driving up Broadway in front of the two places threatened to release another flood of memory. Colter resisted the urge to surrender completely to the past and knock on the door of his grandparents' old house, wondering as he drove by if he might have discovered some missing part of himself still trapped inside. The town seemed smaller, lost in the huge storm sweeping down across western Oklahoma, and everything had gotten much, much older. Grayer. The wind tossed the single blinking red light above the empty four-way stop at Broadway and Main like a tin can on strings. Fairview belied its name. It seemed to Colter as if all the little dried-up town had ever housed were small, troubled souls. He remembered when the flashing stoplight had been added, recalling the frustration his father had felt in just trying to get the town council to spend the money.

Lights were on in the bank, with a late model Chevy parked in one of the alley parking slots. Colter slowed for the four-way stop, glanced both ways, and was about to pull into the deserted intersection when he thought about the nightwatchman. Instead of rolling through, he came to a full, complete stop, but the menacing black pickup was nowhere in sight. Except for a single car parked a half block down Main Street to his left, and a couple of farm trucks angle parked ahead on Broadway, the streets were deserted on this windblown Good Friday. The storefronts along both sides of Main Street were boarded up except for a drugstore on one side, a small grocery on the other. He supposed everybody shopped at the new Wal-Mart at Watonga, twenty miles distant on the interstate.

Who would still live here, he thought. Who could? Cold gusts blasted the snow along deserted sidewalks. With his window down, the wind moaned so loudly in the telephone wires behind the rows of empty storefronts that Colter could hear it above the growl of his engine. He felt old and tired and cold clear through to his bones.

On his first pass north along Broadway, Colter glanced at the old hotel, noticing in a cheerfully lit downstairs window a hand-lettered sign with the single word: Café. Next door to the café an aptly named beer joint named The Beer Joint caught his eye. Judging from the two pickup trucks already parked there in midafternoon, the bar was a thriving enterprise and now occupied the old laundry that had stood next to the hotel for as long as Colter could remember. The matched pair of Ford 150 pickups appeared to be the only sign of life in four intersecting blocks of downtown. The false front of The Beer Joint had been constructed of plywood and painted to look like a mine entrance, some sort of feeble Wild West imagery, with a red and blue neon Budweiser sign that flickered sporadically beside the darkened mine tunnel entrance. Except for the blinking stoplight and the flickering Budweiser sign in the bar window, the town was rendered in stop-action black and white like some grainy Depression-era photograph. As Colter made his quiet pass on the street, the blue and red neon pulsed softly through the falling snow.

Mauldin's Place, the Indian bar across the street, looked unchanged. Windows still boarded up, sidewalk in front littered with windblown trash, a hand-painted sign that simply said "Beer," hanging a little lopsided above the door. Never a sign of life on the street side until the sun went down, and even then all the real action reserved for the alley door. When somebody went into Mauldin's, it was rarely for a front door kind of reason.

On north, the only other color visible in town, in marked counterpoint to The Beer Joint's sign next to the hotel, was a static red neon "Jesus Saves," on the signboard standing in front of the First Baptist Church at the far end of the street. At least it isn't flashing, Colter thought. He imagined the same street scene tomorrow night, with maybe twice as many pickups angle parked along the street in front of The Beer Joint. Later, on Easter Sunday morning, the same pickups, this time alongside a handful of family sedans, would all be found down the street in front of the church.

Far too tired for any Friday night hoopla, Colter thought he would check out the bar on Saturday. By then he was sure everyone in town would know he was back anyway. He pictured smiles, maybe a round of drinks and a little jukebox country and western. Not quite the homecoming he had long imagined. "Not really boating weather anyway," he said to Leon, who was steadfastly snoring away the day.

The Grand Hotel, the only two-story wood-frame building still standing from Fairview's founding days, looked inviting as he drove by, the backlit café sign in the window the single spot of warmth along the street. He had wanted to make a quick swing through town, just to get his bearings, but he couldn't go on. The pull of the cozy light from the little lobby café spilling out onto the sidewalk, the thought of clean sheets, a warm room out of the storm, with a window for chrissake, and not that tomb of a truck, was too much to resist.

He did a quick U-turn at the end of the block, then, after glancing around for the nightwatchman, another abrupt U-turn into the angled parking slot in front of the café.

As soon as he had parked and entered the café, Colter noticed from the round clockface on the wall that his watch was losing time. He shook it a couple of times, enough to jar loose whatever was stuck, but then it stopped again. Right next to the clock hung that same wall calendar again, clear sign of an aggressive Baptist evangelism afoot, and beside the cash register, the same cardboard ring of red paper poppies. He found himself searching the face at the front desk, a frumpy young woman and obviously one of the new owners, for anything familiar, some possible resemblance to Rae Lynn perhaps, but there was none.

The transaction, except for Leon, was simple. Colter was given the bridal suite, the only finished room in the midst of a remodeling project, with strict instructions to keep the dog off the bed. Already midafternoon, the day dark and closed in, Colter grabbed a quick cheeseburger and fries from the little café, then moved the truck around to a vacant lot across the alley and away from the hotel, leaving the engine idling to keep the diesel liquid. He popped the last can of Strongheart for Leon and climbed the back stairs, lugging his overnighter with a change of clothes and urging Leon up each and every one of the nineteen steps. His room was at the far end of a dark hallway above the café and warm from the kitchen, with a trio of tall windows overlooking the street. The light, diffused softly through lace curtains and the gentle sifting of snow, fell across the big four-poster bridal bed. Leon, with a little assistance, curled up at the foot of the big bed in flagrant violation of the rules, and Colter, after shedding his muddy clothes, slipped in between clean sheets and fell immediately into a deep and peaceful sleep.

He awoke only once at Leon's urgent whining for an emergency trip down the back stairs. The snow swirled invisibly through the night sky behind the hotel, but in the cone of yellow light from the pole at the end of the alley Colter could just make out the grill and headlight assembly of a black vehicle parked around the corner. Barefoot, freezing, and Leon through with his business now, he figured knowing for sure just wasn't worth the effort.

૭ Saturday, April 2, 1994

Chapter Fifteen

Saturday morning came around slowly, a pleasant reminder of home after the confusion of the night, and day, and night again since he had left Albuquerque. Soft dawn light filtered through the lace curtains while the smell of frying bacon wafted up through the stairwell onto the second-floor landing and seeped in under the door. With first awareness he looked at his watch. It said 2:15, clearly out of whack with the smell of bacon. The trusty little Timex digital had obviously ticked its last tock. Entropy gaining fast, he thought, and still early morning. Beyond the lace curtains Colter could see only gray overcast, but at least the snow had stopped. The nightwatchman's black truck was nowhere in sight.

In his exhausted afternoon crash, Colter hadn't paid much attention to Leon. Good for Colter, bad for Leon. He vaguely remembered a stumbling emergency trip down the back stairs in the middle of the night, but Leon was already standing at the door, waiting for his morning routine of pee, poop, drink, eat, and poop again. Colter showered quickly, the cold water in the bath down the hall as refreshing as a baptism, and threw on fresh clothes. Once downstairs, not an easy task since Leon actually did better going up than down, Colter checked on the rig, still idling faithfully, and remembered he had used up the last of the dog food yesterday, thinking to visit J & E Grocery right after breakfast.

He was torn between driving back out to the frontage road and Oliver's diner for breakfast, or exploring the little downstairs café. Expedience, an intense desire to avoid a repeat of yesterday morning with the nightwatchman, and the smell of bacon won out. As soon as he had put Leon through his paces, and over mild protests of hunger put him in the cab for his morning nap, Colter went in through the downstairs back door, down the darkened hallway past doorways emptying into empty, unfinished rooms, and emerged into the light again near the front of the hotel.

The last door to the left, into the actual lobby, was locked. Peering through the etched glass, he suddenly remembered a childhood visit to the hotel, the excitement of some after-dark errand with his father, and this very room full of old men sitting quietly, mesmerized by the blue glow of a little round-screened Philco television set. It was the first television Colter had ever seen. He had wanted very much to stay and watch the figures on the little screen, but his father's urgent agenda, whatever it might have been, had prevailed. He could still remember the insistent tug on his hand, the dark hallway. Where the old men had sat so quietly, lost in the warm embrace of that summer evening, he now saw a room piled full of antique furniture. There were a couple of overstuffed wingback chairs with fancy carved legs, the kind that used to dance across the screen in Walt Disney cartoons, at least three old sofas of various flower print fabrics all stacked against one wall, and a tall sideboard with a white marble countertop. On the marble slab stood a large white and blue washbowl and matching pitcher. He looked closer, hoping to see the old, round-screen Philco, but no luck. The room had a dusty look, with faint light coming through the yellowed sheers at the front window. For some reason the place reminded him of a funeral parlor. He remembered Mrs. Adams, an energetic little bee of a woman, feather duster in hand, who had inherited the hotel from her father. When Colter heard the metal sign out front squeaking in the wind on rusty hinges, he half expected to see little Mrs. Adams, with her maid's apron and white hair, trudging up the hallway with an oilcan and ladder. The old people were certainly all gone now, even energetic Mrs. Adams, the jumble of parlor furniture all that remained of their day.

Across the hall, through a new white French door opposite the lobby, Colter could see the little café in what used to be the front two rooms of the hotel, with the kitchen probably converted from the downstairs hall bath, midway back. A clockfaced sign hanging on the door said the place would open at seven, but with his watch fresh out of time, he had to press his face against the glass of the door to see from the wall clock inside that he only had another couple of minutes to wait. He could see light coming from the kitchen end, and through the single-pane glass he could hear running water, the heavy bang of a skillet against a stovetop burner grate, but no one came far enough out front to catch his eye.

Inside, the tables were all round oak kitchen tables of varying sizes, the kind he had grown up with, now probably the stuff of local farm auctions. A few had ornate carved legs, the table nearest the door boasting elaborate lions' paws, a four-legged griffin clutching four glass balls. The chairs were a mishmash of old, straight ladder-backs, and a scattering of cheap captain's chairs from Unpainted Furniture. Altogether the effect was warm and pleasing and in sharp contrast to the slick Denny's style of chrome and plastic along the interstate.

Standing outside in the hall, he could feel a cold draft from the alley door, but the smell of bacon frying came on strong from inside the café. The woman who finally came to the front door at a little after seven was a middle-aged version of the granola type from the day before. Colter found himself holding his breath while he searched her face, but it wasn't Rae Lynn. The woman had gathered her gray hair into a thick braid and wore a long, full, wrinkled green skirt and not quite matching greenish sweater. Sticking out the bottom of the skirt like two white stovepipes were calves of cotton long underwear, which ran from the bottom of the skirt hem down into a pair of ankle-high boots. She was pretty in a comfortable, homey sort of way, so totally unlike Marilyn with her crisp, no-nonsense glamour, that Colter was taken aback. It hadn't occurred to him for years that there was any other kind of pretty, and he wondered in the same second what Rae

Lynn whatever-her-name-was-now might look like. The woman smiled and apologized for keeping their first overnight guest waiting in the cold, Colter quickly figuring her daughter must have been the one who checked him in the day before. After a lazy breakfast of hot oatmeal, bacon, eggs, toast, and coffee, Colter arranged for a second night in the honeymoon suite, paid in advance including a hefty tip, and left to explore, in the gathering light of a new April day, the lost world of his own beginnings. Roots, like Oliver said.

He lifted Leon down out of the cab for the walk and they followed the alley behind the hotel north, behind the row of storefronts, toward where he thought he had seen the black truck in the night, but the street at the end was empty. How small it all seemed now. Just a grubby little High Plains town where no one even remembered him. The air was cold, the sky overcast but with a drier feel to it, the cold more biting, as if the wet, beating heart of the storm had moved on east. He could imagine that patch of blue again, a subtle clearing in the west, some-where off beyond the low horizon below his line of sight. "Probably clear at home right now, Bud," he said to Leon, looking around to make sure no one heard him talking to the dog.

At the place where the alley came out onto Maple Avenue, he looked east toward the Methodist church and beyond, toward the school, and for a moment he felt disoriented, as if the alley he had been familiar with since childhood had conspired with Maple Street to deceive him. The church was gone. He looked east again along Maple, where sure enough the same ancient Chinese elms mingled their branches in a deli-cate arch of winter finery above the street. The parsonage stood just where it should, with its white clapboard siding, the green asphalt shin-gles curling up at the edges now with age, but the colors right, the pro-portions correct as he remembered—the same house certainly.

But the white church next door, the one with the wide gray cement steps and the pipe handrail polished to a pewter luster, was gone. The big white church with the wide, swing-open double doors and the bell rope hanging just to one side of the vestibule where the pigeons cooed softly sometimes during Sunday services, simply wasn't there. In its place was a vacant, weed-grown lot, and Colter could feel his heart sinking. For years his imagined homecoming had touched upon this little white clapboard Methodist church, with its solid white cross and pointed bell tower. Once, on a dare during a particularly boring funeral service for some old woman Colter didn't even know, he had slipped unnoticed out the aisle end of the back pew and swung once off the bell rope that hung in the vestibule. Thinking of it, he could still feel the heavy, vibrating tones of the brass bell resonating in its closed space above the vestibule ceiling, could hear the sudden clatter of the pigeons. He could remember that odd mixture of outrage and amusement on the faces turned his way, could even remember exactly how the rope looked sliding up through the little hole in the ceiling, how it moved silently up and down even after the bell had quit.

Colter had simply expected to round the corner of the alley onto Maple, glance eastward, and there the church would stand. Forever. In one little corner of his mind he had envisioned someday knocking on the parsonage door and asking the current pastor for a quiet tour. It was the church he was raised in. He had gone in and out those double doors from the time of his earliest memories. He would sit nestled safely between his parents on the hard maple pew while high on the east wall the sunlight streamed in through a stained-glass Jesus wearing a purple robe. He remembered, too, those moments of heart-pounding fear, waiting alone in that dark and close and secret space behind the pulpit while a choir of little angels sang their next to last song, his cue to step out in his own purple robe and recite a Christmas poem. And where was the basement? What had they done with the basement, with its lingering smell of tuna casserole and cherry pie from the covered-dish suppers, or the Sunday School rooms, such tiny cubicles after all, as Colter now began to imagine? And those rows of Cradle Roll pictures, each with a little cluster of egg-shaped portraits going all the way back to that ancient, prehistoric time of his mother's childhood, the portrait of her smiling, freckled face and curls hung among the earliest of the early, back near the damp stairwell entrance on the east side. He had been married in that church, for chrissake. How could they have let the church slip away? All this in an instant, the shock of loss an angry, physical one, and he realized that he had stopped dead in his tracks and that Leon was looking up at him with his head cocked sideways, that quizzical look on his old, sagging retriever face. Colter could feel his eyes stinging suddenly from salt water and cold.

Jesus. The earth had just moved beneath his feet, and for a fleeting instant Colter Wayne Tyree felt, as a physical sensation in his chest, the passing rush of time. He walked on, still unbelieving, east along Maple toward the gaping vacant lot, half hoping he had made a mistake, that he was somehow on the wrong street. Crossing in the middle of the block he could see that the church was indeed gone, but not without a trace. What remained was a broken slab of the wide, sweeping front steps leading up from the sidewalk a foot or so into thin air. Too heavy for whatever earthmoving equipment they had brought in, the slab now stepped up into nothingness; not even a foundation outline remained, the basement hole filled in, and only a few scattered, charred board ends poked up through the snow to tell the tale.

And what a conflagration he hoped it was, this burning of his past. In his mind's eye he could see the flames swelling up into the night sky and Fairview's pathetic little antique red fire engine fitfully pumping its contents into the surging light until the spectators, even the volunteer firemen, had to finally retreat. A burn to remember.

Now, standing in the snow beneath a gray April sky that looked more like November, the street cold and empty at his back, Cowboy Colter had to choke back the tears.

can see it.
feel it.

Chapter Sixteen

Only two stores and the corner bank were still occupied along Main Street, and up and down the entire three-block length of Broadway, only a Shamrock station, the hotel, the two bars, and the Baptist church at the far end showed any signs of life. A ghost town. The place looked like a goddamn ghost town.

Colter remembered the Fairview of his childhood as a Saturday kind of town. Farmers in for shopping, haircuts, and ice cream. Merchants having sidewalk sales, maybe a Lion's Club street dance on a summer Saturday night. The old grocery store on Main Street, still open but apparently under new management, was no longer the J & E Grocery he remembered. Same silly fifties false front of aluminum and rusting tin, but now Shea's Grocery. He had known a kid named Shea in school but could not in a thousand years imagine the kind of milk-carton age progression it would take to transform that particular Shea into an actual grown-up grocery store owner. The store stood on the north side of the street directly across from the Fairview Drug, which had the only storefront restored to its original red brick facade up and down the street. Colter promised himself to go across later and compliment the owner on his good taste as well as his courage in the face of <u>Fairview's galloping collapse.</u> But first he went instead into the grocery and bought a fifty-pound bag of Purina dog chow and a case of twenty-four cans of Strongheart in the smaller eight-ounce size.

"Truck driver," he told the aging checker, watching for any sign of recognition. "Travel with my buddy, there." He pointed to Leon waiting patiently on the sidewalk. "We're just waiting out some repairs."

The clerk smiled an amused smile, as if he'd already seen just about everything else, and this was the last thing left. "Stop for him to poop, do you? Always wondered about that. Truckers with pets."

"He's pretty regular, actually," Colter said. "Once in the morning, early, then again about an hour after breakfast, then again sometime around nine or ten at night, but he can hold that one if he has to. Not much trouble, really. Hardest part is picking up the dog food every couple of weeks." Colter left out the part about lifting the beast in and out of the damn truck.

The clerk nodded. "We have a poodle, but Mrs. Grantham spoils him. My wife, Mrs. Grantham."

Colter's turn to nod at the unfamiliar name with some relief while the clerk rang up the purchase. Who the hell was Shea, he wondered. Then he hefted the sack over his left shoulder, gathered the case of cans under his right arm, and pushed his way out the door, Leon following along at his heels and sniffing the sacked Purina all the way back to the truck in the alley behind the hotel.

After a quick and noisy feeding and a slurping of water from the blue water dish on the passenger-side floor, they headed out again, Leon finding just the right spot to conduct his business in a vacant lot near the end of the block.

Still shaken by the missing church, Colter dreaded further disappointment. Things were sure as hell not what they had been when he <u>left thirty years ago.</u> Back on Main Street and eager for a little human companionship, he tied Leon to the light pole in front of the drugstore. Once inside, he sensed a furtive glance of irritation from behind a pair of really thick glasses while the ancient druggist replaced the latest *Time* on the magazine rack, then retreated for some idle task behind the counter.

"Morning," the man said. "Can I help you find anything?"

"Thanks. Just coffee, if it's made." Colter expected to attract a certain amount of attention when someone finally recognized him, but up to now, except for Oliver, the only people he had encountered were complete strangers. God only knew why this one had landed in Fairview. The druggist seemed lost in himself, drawing a fragrant cup of fresh, hot coffee from a tall chrome machine in a mindless, automatic sort of way until Colter thought the coffee might just spill out all over the counter. Just before disaster struck, the druggist looked up suddenly and caught Colter staring.

"Do I know you?" the man asked.

"Sorry," Colter said, suddenly aware of his heartbeat at the mere possibility of recognition. Oliver was clearly onto something with that praise or absolution business. "Rude to stare like that. I was trying to figure out if I knew you, maybe."

"You're from around here?"

"Long time ago," he said. He was actually hoping by now to at least see someone he knew. Somebody who remembered him.

"How long is a long time?" the druggist asked. It was a friendly question, not at all probing.

"A quarter of a century, more or less."

"That's a long time, all right," he said. "Yessir, when you put it that way, that's a long time. Lost my wife almost twenty-five years ago. Guess I never stopped to think of it as a quarter century. I came here about ten years ago, so I couldn't possibly know you. Thought a small town would be a good retirement idea." He smiled a wry smile.

"Sorry," Colter said. "Again. I didn't mean to get you thinking on it." "On it?" Jesus. There went those language skills out the window again. He could already feel himself slipping back into the rhythm of the place.

"Any family still here?" the druggist asked.

"No," Colter said. "Not anymore." He didn't exactly know why, but now the idle questions began to make him nervous. He had nothing to hide, really, except the total failure of his life, and he suddenly felt that if he kept talking much more he would begin to tell this perfect stranger the whole sorry story. This was not what he had in mind for the morning either.

The druggist didn't say anything more, apparently content with the silence. Colter asked for a warm-up on his coffee. Then, unable to resist, he said, "My folks had the bank here."

"That right." Flat. Zero interest.

"Finally got to the point Dad said either he could run the sonofabitch or the federal government could run the sonofabitch, but they couldn't both run the sonofabitch. Something like that."

"Know what he meant," said the druggist, smiling again.

"So he sold out," Colter said. "Some outsider came in, ran the place right into the ground. No offense. The outsider part."

"None taken, son." He waved it off. "Ten years doesn't make you a local. Not in a place like this."

"I was already long gone by that time, so I don't really know much about it, but I guess the new guy and the federal government couldn't run it either, because it finally went belly-up. And took a few investors with it, so I heard. Shame, too. That bank was in our family since before statehood."

"You must be that Tyree boy what up and left. Truth be told, they blame you a little around here for your daddy selling out in the first place. Just talk. You know how it is."

"What kind of talk?" Colter asked, interested now.

"Oh, not much. This and that. But I knew your daddy, and I know he sold out from sheer disgust. Had nothing to do with you not wanting to step up and run it. Just sick of it all. And I can certainly see why," he said, his gesture taking in the view of the deserted street, the row of boarded-up storefronts across the way, the telephone lines swaying in the wind. "I serve on the town council, what there is of it. There's only three of us now, and the mayor, so the mayor gets two votes, and instead of spending a little on potholes, he hires somebody to protect our trashcans from coyotes. Odd priority, you ask me. By the way, have you encountered our latest law enforcement official?"

"Oh, yeah," Colter nodded. The question caught him off guard, his broadside alert suddenly going off.

"Truth is, I'm convinced the man's dangerous. Hope you didn't have a real run-in with him. I believe he's a liability for the town, but I'm probably saying more than I should."

There was a tone of sincerity that allowed for a cautious lowering of Colter's guard, and so he described briefly his impression of the man based on the two encounters, carefully omitting any reference to grave robbing or unregistered firearms.

"I'm afraid the man's a loose cannon," said the druggist. He smiled. "That phrase, by the way, refers back to when cannon were wheel mounted for mobility but chained in place on the wooden deck. Nothing worse than a two-ton cannon broken loose from its mooring chain in a storm. Could do a lot of damage very quickly. I'm an old navy man myself. You were in the service, too, weren't you?"

"Strange, the bank still there and not there," Colter said, quickly changing the topic away from his service record. He enjoyed a momentary vision of the nightwatchman, all three hundred pounds of him, dead and stiff and heavy as a cannon crashing through a bridge rail and pitching headfirst into a shallow sandbank below.

"My dad was the one pushed for all these aluminum false fronts back in the fifties," he said. "Ruined the look of the place, you ask me. I like what you did to this one."

"Tell you the truth, I kind of liked that fifties look, but the damn thing blew loose in a storm the year after I took over the place."

Not much common ground there. The family bank was a real sore point with Colter. He kept quiet to avoid sounding like a petulant child to the druggist, but that hideous two-story false aluminum front drove him crazy. It seemed as if the bank and its honest red brick masonry of ninety years ago were trapped behind the grillwork of an oversize Buick. His father's legacy. Somewhere Colter had seen an old photograph of the original bank. In the faded sepia tone his grandmother sat in an open upstairs window, posing for the photographer with her wide skirts bunched and visible, her head held high and proud, while his grandfather stood below, next to his horse tied to the hitching post beside the front door. They looked such a proud young couple, and it had been their bank. True, the first lie had been to extend the brick parapet above the actual roofline in a square facade, making the building appear taller by three or four feet than it really was. But for some reason he could forgive his grandfather. Colter's father, both bank president and president of the chamber of commerce, installed the aluminum false fronts a half century later. El Jefe, Colter thought. The Man. A surge of petty jealousy, then, Colter realizing he had never been president of anything except a failed freight business.

"Nothing goes on forever, son," the druggist said heavily, as if his remarks contained some profound and lasting truth. On that note Colter finished his coffee and paid at the counter.

Later, walking the deserted sidewalks around town, Colter began to realize just how little went on forever. After the drugstore, everywhere Colter went along the deserted streets, he felt the push-pull of past and present. Sometimes the easiest thing was just to stand still and take in a certain view, remember a smell, like the smell of fresh hot bread filtering out onto the sidewalk through the screen door of Blood's Bakery. When he walked up the sidewalk on the north side of Main Street he simply expected to smell the bread without consciously thinking about the bakery at all, so strongly was the smell of bread associated with that side of the street in his childhood.

The storefront that had been the bakery was boarded up behind four large sheets of plywood, and they looked as if they had been in place for a while. Hieroglyphics of graffiti, layered through time, covered most of the plywood. The earliest layer readable, harking back to a simpler age, read "Go Seniors '72." A similar inscription, visible from the highway on the southeast side of the round water tower, suggested 1972 as the peak year for verbal skills, perhaps the end of the age of innocence for his tiny hometown. The overlaying graffiti appeared indecipherable as a foreign language. His first impulse was to feel singled out, as if there might be some grand conspiracy to deprive him of those feelings he was entitled to upon coming home. Then he realized how many others must have returned to find things gone or changed so completely they might as well have stayed gone. He could imagine all the old dead and departed lined up at the river's edge, waiting their turn to come back across and find the place empty of all they remembered.

Disappointed, he walked on slowly west along Main Street, each sight triggering a universe of remembered smells and echoing sounds. Leon, untroubled by ghosts, paused at each light pole to mark his passing with his own particular kind of graffiti. Colter's walk finally became a game of deciding which memories to savor, which impressions to squander, knowing as he made each decision that the right now of his first homecoming would never come again.

Chapter Seventeen

From the looks of it, the storefront office of the *Fairview Democrat* had been boarded up for years. He remembered the sales and advertising office and the old typesetting machine up toward the front, and the giant press, a nightmare of a machine that took up almost all of the print shop at the back. There were huge ceramic crucibles where dull ingots of lead alloy were melted down to pour into the flat trays of type plates. He remembered, too, the smothering dark beneath a couple of low-watt bulbs, the filth and grime, as if it were not a place of enlightenment at all. Rather the back shop seemed to house a keeper whose job it was simply to feed the clanging black monster that stood in the middle of the darkened, low-ceilinged room and destroyed lives. Colter remembered the newspaperman coming to the front wearing a filthy, ink-covered apron he had used to crudely clean his hands. It seemed to Colter that the man had only so much truth in him, with little left over for the gulping mouth and throat of his monster enterprise, for it was this man and his rumbling black machine that in the end had caused his family such pain.

It was the year Johnny Lonewolf lied about his age and ran off to join the navy. Not long after, classes let out for the summer, and by fall

Oliver was already on the school superintendent's radar for truancy. The next time Colter saw him he was sitting on the bank corner, nursing a sacked bottle of cheap Thunderbird port in the afternoon shade along with the rest of the leftover Cheyenne.

Oliver was still sitting on the bank corner, watching time pass, that fall afternoon when Colter's father came out of the café located diagonal across the four-way stop, pushing Oliver's drunken stepfather ahead of him—carrying him really—by the shirt collar and the seat of his pants, out the door and down the sidewalk toward the jail. The charge would have been drunk and disorderly at worst, if anybody back then had even bothered with formal charges against a drunk white man. The customary punishment was to just let them sleep it off out of harm's way, but Colter remembered that night as the night that changed things forever. They found Oliver's stepfather the next morning hanging by his own belt from the top crossbar on his cell door. It was a sloppy job. The man had slowly strangled instead of neatly breaking his neck. His death was ruled a suicide, but in that town, in that time, who could know for sure.

In the aftermath the newspaperman, fella name of Hermann, made a big deal about the legality of a citizen's arrest, implying that what Clinton Tyree had done was not far removed from a one-man lynch mob, in form if not in fact. The newspaper publisher and Colter's father had been political adversaries for years, the one a Stevenson democrat living across the state, and Colter's father an Eisenhower republican, seen in the political spectrum of a borderline democratic county as just a little to the right of Attila the Hun.

There was never any real suspicion that Colter's father had anything directly to do with the man's death, but after the publisher's attack Colter's father never really forgave himself for his part in the tragedy and later even tried to reimburse the county for burial expenses, which only made things worse. Colter, remembering the pain and shame he had seen in his childhood friend's face, had never really forgiven his father either. By that time Colter was already alert for things to fault his father for, and looking back, the episode had probably marked the beginning of the end for both of them.

Colter half expected the editor to come to the front, wiping his guilty hands again, but the door was locked. A quick, self-conscious peek through a sliver of front window revealed a black nothing.

Colter quickly stood away from the window and looked around, but the early morning sidewalk, cold and blown with snow, was as empty as the one in that Johnny Cash song. The jail where Oliver's stepfather had hanged himself was a low, squat, block building around the corner. It faced onto the alley next to the fire station just across from the back door of the newspaper office. The city offices fronted on the other street, with the jail added on as an afterthought, Colter remembered, to replace the old concrete bunker that sat for years at the edge of the park. Ironic that his father had been responsible for that civic improvement, too, arguing that the old jail of puddled concrete and iron doors, sitting exposed on the hillside above the city park, was too hot in summer and too cold by far in winter. Clearly a man ahead of his time in prison reform.

Counting ahead, Colter figured the fourth alley door on his right would be the newspaper office, immediately next to the back door of the pool hall just beyond. The sense of trespass made the hair stand up on his neck as he gently tried the door. It gave a little as he pushed, Colter still not aware exactly what truth he might be seeking with a look at the old press. At the same moment, out of the corner of his eye, he spotted an approaching figure wrapped in a frayed old army-issue wool blanket. The creature came staggering down the alley from the vicinity of Mauldin's back door as if he had already been hard at it on a Saturday morning. Whiskey Indian.

Colter stopped in his tracks, thinking that if he didn't move, the Indian might not see him at all. Bad as Gallup, he thought. When the Indian staggered toward them Leon began wagging his tail. The Indian seemed to veer off a little when he noticed the dog but sheer momentum kept him going another step or two beyond, toward the back wall of the newspaper office. Finally Colter had to reach down and gently take Leon by the scuff of the neck to keep the whole thing from getting out of hand. The dog looked up quickly, pulled his floppy retriever ears back for a second, then looked back at the deflected Indian, tail still wagging.

"Hey, white man," the Indian said in a low mumbled growl, lurching to an unsteady halt. "Spare some change?"

The drunk, his face hidden by the hood of the draped blanket and a pair of dark sunglasses, wasn't looking directly at Colter, but stared instead off toward the end of the alley. The blanket had been pulled up over his head to form the hood, then the right side had been wrapped back up over his left shoulder like an army poncho. He seemed to be having trouble focusing and standing upright at the same time, and he kept bobbing and weaving and craning his neck as if he had lost track of something very important and was trying hard to find it again. Beneath the blanket his arms appeared to be held out from his sides like a wounded bird's wings for balance.

Colter moved slowly away from the back door of the newspaper office, trying to disassociate himself from the Indian, the alley, the entire episode. He started to say something witty, something about a hair off the dog that bit you, something along those lines, but feeling the handful of loose skin and hair on the back of Leon's neck, he thought better of it. Instead, out came a practiced "Sorry, no change."

The Indian just looked at his spot on the wall, as if Colter were really over there somewhere. Except for having stopped all forward motion, the Indian had not acknowledged Leon at all. Suddenly the Indian gathered his arms back into himself and turned just enough to the side for a profile view. He pulled the blanket up out of the way, pawed at his fly for a second, and then began to urinate out of the longest whang Colter had ever seen. He felt an embarrassed urge to look away but sheer fascination prevailed while he listened to the sound of a cow pissing on a flat rock. A bathtub filling. Niagara.

Turning unsteadily away, the Indian made a feeble attempt to cage the monster back inside his unbuttoned fly. "Don't make 'em like that anymore, huh, white man?" he mumbled.

"Let's go, boy," Colter said, turning away and pulling on Leon's neck fur at the same time. Walking slowly away, Colter could feel the Indian's stare on the back of his neck, but when he glanced back from the end of the alley the Indian had disappeared.

Being caught prying at the back door of the old newspaper office by anyone, even a drunk Indian, made Colter uneasy. Leon whined, straining to pull away from Colter's firm grip and return to the alley as they rounded the corner and headed back to Main Street. The old place has sure enough gone to hell, Colter thought, crossing the empty street. He didn't have to look both ways to know there was no traffic coming.

The drugstore was beginning to look like the only diversion available, but glancing in the front window he saw the massive bulk and head of the nightwatchman sitting in the far booth, back to the window. And no sign of the pickup, either. Sly bastard. Probably parked out back.

On impulse Colter tied Leon to the streetlight in front and went on in, nodding a polite greeting. So what if he'd had a couple of close calls out on the road, a near miss with a weapons charge, and had just been interrupted at the start of a minor break and enter by a drunk Indian, and this was only day two. What the hell, push the envelope a little. He'd been raised in this town, and by God he could have a cup of coffee in the drugstore just as well as the next guy.

After a while it was clear no one else was coming in. Aside from a little strained chatter about the cold, which didn't take long to get through, it was clear the three of them didn't have much to say to each other. Colter, unwilling to put himself through any more of it, waved off the pharmacist bringing a refill, paid his coffee tab, and walked out, nodding politely to the nightwatchman's impassive backside as he left.

Chapter Eighteen

Sure starting to look like a long weekend.

By late Saturday afternoon Colter had seen everything in the old burg he wanted to see. Last night's sleep had been better than any in recent memory, but a wide yawn at the curb said Leon was ready to crash again.

On his way to the hotel the flickering blue and red beer sign beside the entrance to the mine shaft worked its magic. Maybe just one, he thought. After all, it wasn't like he was really on the road or anything. Colter tied Leon to the back porch rail of the hotel, wolfed down a "cheeseburger to go" between the café door and the end of the hall, then helped Leon up into the cab, figuring the odds for an accident-free nap were better there than unattended in the bridal suite.

In his entire claustrophobic life, Colter had never actually set foot inside a mine shaft, but once inside the bar he figured this was how dark it must be. Recessed lighting above an old, mirrored backbar highlighted a lot of ornate woodwork. A pathetic little collection of baseball caps hung from the ceiling, and a handful of dollar bills, each with a scrawled signature, were pinned onto a bulletin board beside the bar. Colter supposed it was some kind of hedge against really hard times when the last five people in town could claim a beer on their way out. Clearly somebody had bet the farm on a little spillover prosperity from the lake, or maybe a flurry of oil and gas activity, and had gone to a lot of trouble and expense to set the place up. The bar ran almost a third the length of the place, with tables in front, an honest-to-god sawdust dance square and raised bandstand at the far back, and a row of high-back booths along the opposite wall to the right. No bartender in sight, but with the door unlocked Colter thought maybe the guy was in the back taking a leak. The booths were designed for privacy, so he couldn't be sure, but in the dim light Colter couldn't see any customers at this early hour, despite the two trucks parked out front.

He took a seat in the booth closest to the door. No noisy jukebox at this hour, but subdued voices from somewhere in the back. Now that he thought about it, Colter was a little relieved the place was still empty. He couldn't imagine coming in later, the place hopping full of people he knew in his heart of hearts he really didn't want to see. Colter was already starting to think this was probably a bad idea anyhow when a tall, lanky old fellow in faded Levi's, a faded blue down jacket with frayed cuffs, rubber overshoes, and a sweat-stained John Deere cap strode out from the back hall bathroom. He stopped short, saying over his shoulder toward the storeroom, "Damned if you ain't got a customer out here, Al."

In a heartbeat Colter realized who it was.

"Sonofabitch," the man said, stopping in midstride toward the door. "Look what the cat drug in." The bartender, a young guy with an apron, poked his head around the storeroom door.

Colter had been waiting for this. Dreading it. In fact, if he thought about it, he had been dreading this moment for most of his adult life. The old guy was still remarkably fit looking. Tall, handsome with a thin face and neatly trimmed white mustache. Old bastard probably still had a full shock of white hair hid under the John Deere cap. Looked like the goddamn Marlboro man before the cancer got him. Had to be eighty-something if he was a day.

"Oney," Colter nodded.

"Jesus, boy, what a thing you done."

No pleasantries. Right to the point. Colter braced himself for the moment. This was the one. Colter had always known it would be this one person. Oney McRae. Crying shame the goddamn truck wasn't ready yet.

"What thing's that, Oney?" Colter looked up into the shadow beneath the John Deere hat at the man's heavy eyebrows.

"Why, leaving like that, so sudden an' all. I heard you never even said good-bye or howdy do to your friends. Nothing. Can't stand the heat, get out of the kitchen. That about sum it up?"

Colter didn't say anything. He had learned that. At least that. The bartender stayed discretely in the storeroom but left the door ajar, the light slicing across the dark hall floor in front of the bathrooms.

"Caused quite a stir round these parts, rich kid like you taking off without a word."

Wanting to get it all out and over with at once, Colter kept quiet.

"That note was a piece of work. I'll give you that."

"Note?" Colter tried too late to compose himself.

A second's pause. "There never even was a fucking note," Oney said, amazed. "They made that one up, didn't they. To save face. Christ, boy, you ought to be horsewhipped for leaving like that. Never mind what it did to my Rae Lynn."

He was an old man now. Colter had thought he was old already when he was just Rae Lynn's dad, but now he was *really* old.

"I don't know, Oney. That was, let's see, by my calculations about thirty years ago. She seemed pretty okay to me, her eyes on the quarterback at the time."

"He turned out to be a sorry sonofabitch too." Now Oney just looked away, his blue eyes watery with age above slightly quavering thin lips. Then he seemed to see Colter for the first time. "She never did have no luck."

Still all cowboy, Colter thought, but old as dirt now. Not exactly harmless, but less a threat than he once was. Colter didn't ask him to sit down. Part of why Colter never came back was standing over him right now. One piece of why he held his breath every time he roared by on the interstate, so few miles from this very place.

"She still live around here?"

"They never knew, did they? They never even knew what happened to you. Couldn't face it. All those years, and they had to make shit up. Jesus Christ but you're a piece of work. Maybe Rae Lynn had a little luck after all."

"They knew," Colter said. "Guess I just wasn't much to brag about."

The old man looked at him, lower lip and square jaw still quivering. "He and your granddaddy meant everything to this town, never mind that damn newspaper. We had a crowd, I'd raise a beer to 'em both right now. What I want to know, how could you not even show up for your own daddy's funeral service?"

Colter just stared at the little bottle rings and cigarette burns on the tabletop. He really had no idea how to answer that one. Clueless still, for all the times he'd thought about it.

"Hope you had a nice life, boy." With that the old man turned and walked steadily away, going out with a sudden blast of cold that Colter could feel all the way from the street.

"Thanks, Oney. That makes me feel real good now. Surely does," Colter said to the empty barroom, the closed door.

The bartender, a true professional and nonjudgmental as the best of them, never once came out of the storeroom. Colter figured him for just another stranger anyway. So much for a homecoming celebration. No fatted cow for Cowboy Colter. He waited a couple of minutes, watching the big hand on the Coors clock, then dropped a dollar tip for booth rent at the end of the bar and left.

Christ, it was going to be a long weekend.

Chapter Nineteen

Not even dark yet, and Mauldin's, just across the street, already in full swing.

Colter had heard the jukebox from the second he stepped out of the mine shaft, but when he crossed over and opened the door, the sound of Elvis crooning "Heartbreak Hotel" hit him like a wall. The music blared out of a classic old Wurlitzer, the thing all bright lights and sparkles and noise like some miniature spaceship landed smack up against the south wall. The jukebox wailed along at about ninety decibels, completely out of sync with the Michael Jackson video playing silently at nearly life size on a big screen TV mounted high on the back wall above the shuffleboard table.

When Colter was a little kid, the place had always reeked of menace. Knife fights and who knew what else went on there. It was always dark inside, the music always loud, spilling out on the street. Later on, but before Oliver's old man and the bad stuff at the river and then the bus trip west on 66, he and his friends could usually count on a few Indians standing around the alley door on hot summer nights. Easy enough to get one of them to go back inside and hand you a six-pack or a pint of orange-flavored vodka for a buck tip. The alley was dark as a tunnel too, except for a bare low-wattage bulb over the back door of the pool hall a few yards away. The area around the doorway always stunk like piss, and once Colter had even heard the moaning of an urgent coupling from somewhere beyond the reach of light. His father had once compared Mauldin's to the safety valve on a water heater.

Maybe because of the awful weather, the place was filling fast. Colter slid into the only empty booth, the one nearest the door where the cold hit anytime the door opened. He settled in facing the room, his back safely against the wall next to the front door. "Bud," he called out over the wailing music, and the owner, a much older Mauldin who showed no signs of recognition, brought him a tall Bud with the sweat dripping off it, the beer cold enough to crack a tooth.

Shortly two more Indians came into the bar, and at the still early spring hour of approaching dusk, one of them was already too drunk to stand.

The tall one, pockmarked in the face, ageless, with oily black hair down to his shoulders and a thin nose that made him look a little like a hawk, stood looking, sharp eyed, around the bar. His glance hit Colter once, lightly, skimmed over the Indian crowd around the shuffleboard table, and came back to rest on Colter. The short one was stubby as a fireplug, with a spiked gray Mohawk, silver hoop earrings similar to Oliver's, and almost no neck. With the hair beginning to grow out on the sides, the Mohawk was starting to lose its effect, his appearance no more alarming now than some small, furry animal. He bobbed and weaved to an invisible wind, and while Colter watched him, the tall one watched Colter with a hard set of cold black eyes. The tall one didn't appear drunk at all.

Their arrival caused a mild stir among the shuffleboard crowd. They both wore unpolished black combat boots with their camouflage pants tucked in, airborne style, but Colter knew instantly the boots were from some army surplus store down at the city, not the high-top Cochran jump boots issued to jump-qualified personnel.

The milder mannered set had hunkered down near the front of the place where they could either get to the dance floor or get out the front door in a hurry. The rowdy youngsters and one old drunk hanging around the shuffleboard and pool tables in back made most of the noise. Their laughter rose and fell with a subtle rhythm from the clack of the pool balls. On the wall above the last table, a round clock stuck in the middle of a plastic Coors waterfall of pure, Rocky Mountain spring water said it was only 4:37 in the afternoon.

Colter wiped the sweat from the beer with the sleeve of his jacket and set the bottle back down in its own ring of water on the scarred booth top. He sat alone, a white island in a sea of brown that ebbed and flowed around him like so much harmless brown water. For the most part they didn't seem to notice him. Just another truck driver who had mistakenly chosen the wrong bar. No big deal. After the first five minutes he began to wonder what the big deal had ever been, why the Indian bar had always looked so dangerous, so mysterious from the outside. He had been in bars all across the country, mostly since he started driving, and this one was no different from a hundred others. A little more dirt tracked in onto the floor maybe, a little stronger smell of spilled beer and sweat. And the bathroom, well, he was a little reluctant to try the bathroom. But otherwise, just another bar. Colter felt a tiny bit disappointed.

The tall Indian had finally looked away, satisfied that he hadn't backed off looking at this white honky truck driver motherfucker. He gently steered his mohawked friend, who had yet to focus on anything, toward an occupied booth just downwind of the shuffleboard table. The short one raised two fingers in a victory sign and Mauldin right away brought out two cans of Coors regular.

It was clear to Colter that the tall one was definitely not drunk and would bear watching. Very discreetly. Colter had learned that lesson early, and the hard way. No lingering eye contact. He finished his first Bud and ordered a second while a few more Indians drifted into the place through the alley door. Saturday night was warming up, and before he knew it, the place was standing-room only. The noise level had risen, the voices twisted by Cheyenne accents that some of the older ones had picked up long ago at home and never lost. The waterfall moved ceaselessly in the Coors clock on the wall, a silent cascade of mountain stream falling in a rippling light of blue plastic, and while the water fell, time seemed to stand still. Colter was on his fourth Bud when a thin Indian woman of indeterminate age appeared out of nowhere and slid into the booth across from him, tossing down a pack of Virginia Slims.

"I never seen you before," she said.

"Nope," he said, a little wary. "Probably not."

"That your truck over behind the hotel?"

"Yes, Ma'am, it is," Colter said in his best truck driver drawl. There was something familiar about this one, he thought, but he couldn't quite put a name to her. Above-the-knee skirt and a black tank top in this weather. Frankly, a little shopworn for the outfit, too. Colter hoped she had a coat stashed somewhere. He was pretty sure he had gone to high school, or at least junior high, with this one. Birdwing, maybe. One of the Birdwing girls. Age was tough to call through the tracks of a hard life. He remembered how old Oliver's aunt had looked when he was a child, and now, nearly forty years later and probably on her deathbed, she looked as if she had hardly aged at all. This one was going fast, though. Be lucky to live out the decade. Against his will he remembered the one who hadn't. Then, just as quickly, he put that old picture back on the shelf.

"Buy her a beer, white man," said Fireplug. He had turned in his seat and was smiling from two booths away, but from the blank look in his eyes, Colter couldn't even be sure he was being seen clearly. The tall one reached across and nudged Fireplug to shut up.

"That a sleeper cab?" she asked.

"Yes, Ma'am, it is."

"I been in one of those before," she said, and Colter couldn't tell for sure if she was expressing a little pride and worldliness, or simply starting her sales pitch. When she talked he noticed the dark spaces behind the front row of teeth. Like looking in a horse's mouth, he thought. To tell just how old a horse you're looking at before the bucking starts.

"You got a bathroom in there?"

"Nope. No bathroom. More like camping out." He could feel a definite swing toward sales pitch. There was no detectable change in the roll of conversation, the brown faces drifting in and out of his field of vision while the Budweiser did its work and he patiently listened to the woman, but through it all he caught a moment of eye contact with the hawk-faced Indian in the front booth, and it was not a pleasant moment. Colter averted his eyes and felt as though he had done it just in time. She was putting food on the table for someone, all right. Colter was sure of that. Hawkface didn't like it, but he wasn't about to interfere.

"Been lotta miles in that truck, I bet," she said.

"Lotta miles. I live in the damn thing, too."

"I been lotta miles too," she said, grinning quickly at her own joke. "Never been a mile in one those trucks, though."

"No?" Colter said, playing along. "Bet you been a mile or two in a Buick."

"Yeah. Buick." She raised one arm high over her head, exposing a woolly underarm, and for a moment Colter thought she might be giving someone a signal, but it turned out to be no more subtle than ordering another Bud. Testing the water, seeing if Colter would spring for a beer, if nothing else.

"Been around the world in a Buick," she said, and this time she laughed out loud.

Colter half expected one of the beefier Indians to suddenly appear at his side, but the only one who showed up was Mauldin, the bartender.

"What'll it be, Maggie?"

Colter remembered Mauldin as mean enough to run the place. A man who took very little shit off rich, underage white kids who tried to sneak in the back door and cause trouble, or worse yet, hang around the alley waiting for contraband booze. He had aged, but he still had the same hardass look about him. Colter wondered if he was about to be recognized after all.

"One for me, one for the lady. What was your name again, Ma'am?"

"This here's Prairie Flower," said the bartender without cracking a smile. He headed back toward the bar. The man clearly had a sincere respect for honest business negotiations.

"Asshole," said Prairie Flower under her breath as he walked away. "Thinks 'cause he owns my place of business, he owns me."

Probably gets a cut, thought Colter. Funny lady. Smart, good sense of humor, very pretty once, if she really was one of those Birdwing girls. Couldn't remember their first names, but he could almost see the résumé: Name: Prairie Flower; Position Sought: Missionary; Job Experience: Extensive.

Prairie Flower excused herself and headed for the ladies' room.

Killing time now, glancing around the bar through a haze of smoke and his own beer-brained fog, it still broke Colter's heart the way booze and poverty and violence, and sometimes just sheer indifference and neglect, used these people up. As a boy, sneaking a peek into their lives, he had blundered into a place he had no business being, had crawled up close enough to evil that the scent had never left him. It was already too late to help the girl; the man who Colter was sure had committed the outrage had long since fled. Colter was so profoundly disturbed by what he had seen and by his own unintended role in the horror of it that in shock and fear he had carried the secret away with him. In the weeks and months afterward, waiting for the news that never came, he could not imagine why no one had found her, until it finally occurred to him that no one was looking. He was only a boy at the time, but in the end the fact that no one even seemed to miss her overshadowed the horror of her death, compounding his guilt tenfold. The invisible squaw. No one even seemed to know she was gone. He had never gone near that stretch of river again, although in his mind he could still retrace each step that had led him there, each silent footfall as he left. To this day he had never told anyone, unofficial exile and some very bad dreams his only penance. And at this late date he couldn't imagine how to make it right.

Out of the corner of his eye he could still see Hawkface watching. He knew better than to look, but he could feel the Indian's stare against the side of his head. Fireplug sat with his back to them, his fuzzy spike almost motionless. Not drunk. Stoned. Colter was thinking about what clever something to say to Prairie Flower when she returned, engage in a little harmless repartee, when he noticed a sudden drop in the noise level.

Silence moved like a wave from the shuffleboard table near the narrow, back hallway, through the line of stools at the bar, and all the way to Colter's frontline booth. For the first time in what had seemed hours, Hawkface had averted his stare. Fireplug sat still as a fireplug, his spike hairdo erect, motionless in the booth. As Colter looked toward the back he could just see for a moment, caught in the shine of the light above the back door, the black flowing shape of a long, dark overcoat filling the doorway, the nightwatchman sliding out of it to hang the coat on a nail beside the door. He disappeared from sight into the bathroom opposite the storeroom. The man had come in the back door of the bar as quietly as a cat, yet every soul in the place knew of his presence within seconds. The Indians were all looking at the back door now. They had quit their friendly, noisy shuffleboard game as suddenly as if whatever had wound them up for Saturday night had suddenly run down. They all stood there a moment and then began to drift away like smoke, the glow from the Coors light fixture reflecting off the stainless steel puck and the smooth sawdust run of the deserted table.

Someone had just put another quarter in the jukebox, and now Hank Williams Jr. was belting out lyrics about all his rowdy friends to an absolutely silent beer joint. There was a muffled conversation from the back, the sounds of a short scuffle, then a dull thud and glass breaking, but no one made a move to interfere. Colter started to get up out of the booth, but before he had time to think, Hawkface was passing by on his way toward the front door, making eye contact and shaking his head "no," but friendly, as if they were suddenly allies, and Colter was being given fair warning. He would never have guessed the man could move so quickly.

"Motherfucker's early tonight," said one of the Indians who had moved away from the back door shuffleboard when it all began.

"Tomorrow's Easter," another one said, "man's gonna turn in early."

Some of the other Indians standing around silently glared at the two talking, making it clear they should shut up. After an eternity of Hank Jr., Colter got up out of the booth and, to his own astonishment, began to move toward the back hall and the rising voices coming from the bathroom side. He had no earthly idea what he was going to see, nor any idea what he might do about it, but he knew, just as before, that he had to go. The Indians who had moved silently away from the shuffleboard table now backed farther away, making a passageway for Colter to the back hall, where a slow-moving shadow spilled out from the lighted bathroom onto the hall floor. He stopped dead still beside the door, the dim light from a bare bulb over the sink revealing, beyond the massive, thrusting form of the nightwatchman, an upside-down woman. She was bent over the toilet, skirt turned inside-out and hanging nearly to her neck, hands resting lightly on the tank and blood dripping from beneath her cascading hair as if the man was simply holding her up by the waist, gently supporting her against his massive, rocking thighs while she bled from the nose. For only the second time in his life, Colter felt himself in the presence of actual Evil, knowing right then it could come around by train or pickup truck. And just as before, too close to the flame, he took a step back.

At the sound of Colter's footfall in the hall the man half turned, paused in midthrust. They looked at one another for a split second, the nightwatchman taken as much aback by the sight of the unexpected white man as if Colter had been a ghost. And then he smiled his broad, confident smile.

"Everywhere I look," he said.

"Truck's still broke," Colter said, disgusted with his own fear of this man. "She hurt bad?"

"She'll be fine. You might want to wait outside though. If you don't mind. We'll be along in a minute."

Seconds later Colter heard the sound of the woman slumping to the floor, then the big man stepped into the hall, casually buttoning the fly on his overalls and pulling the bathroom door to behind him, shutting down the light. He glanced up front toward the bar, still smiling, then turned and took his overcoat off the nail.

"I wouldn't concern myself too much with this if I were you," he said. "Wouldn't want any official notice brought to bear on that little gun of yours, now would we?"

The hall too confined, too dark now, the man far too close.

"What gun would that be, officer?" Colter said, backing into the dim light of the bar. Drawing a line. Colter had seen this brand of evil before, a lifetime ago, both creatures cut from the same unholy cloth, and he didn't want to ever stand that close again. "Don't own a gun. Never did."

Smiling all the while, the nightwatchman stepped out the back door into the darkened alley, his turn so fast that the heavy overcoat whirled out like a small tent, filling the narrow hall with its black shape. No one else made a move for the bathroom. The Indians all stood around quietly, listening to the raucous sound of Hank Jr. while silence leaked out around the crack of the door onto the narrow hallway floor. Finally a low moan from behind the door, then the sound of something settling, a bottle rolling harmlessly across the floor, then more silence until Colter couldn't stand it anymore.

He regained the couple of steps toward the parted door with a sense of dread that weighed about a thousand pounds, then reached around and flipped the light back on. The nightwatchman had probably caught the woman still seated on the toilet, her panties down around her knees. She couldn't have weighed in over ninety pounds, and it looked as if the bastard had simply stepped in and hit her full in the face. She was bleeding out of her nose and mouth, and the blood had spilled out across her front and begun to pool on the plank floor beneath her face.

"This woman's hurt," Colter shouted. "Somebody get a doctor!" But no one made a move to help her. Colter bent over and tugged her skirt back down, careful not to touch the black garment around her ankles. He looked around for the bartender but couldn't see him for the crowd of wooden Indians just outside the narrow hall.

"That's what happens, you work the wrong side of the street," somebody finally said.

"Is anybody going to call a doctor?" Colter asked again, staying with it this time.

"Don't have one in town, and this sure ain't worth an ambulance ride to Watonga," said the bartender, suddenly at Colter's side. "Couple days, she'll be fine." He moved into the bathroom beside Colter, bringing a cold bar rag, and began to sponge up the blood off the floor. The woman lay moaning, nearly unconscious, beside his knee. She began to stir, then, and finally one of the Indians who had been playing shuffleboard came toward the door.

"Better take her on outa here, Leroy," said the owner. "Looks like she's out of work a day or two at least."

There was no irony or humor intended. Just a simple statement, and it took a moment for the real meaning of it to sink in. Colter wanted to throw up. He could taste the bile rising in his throat, feel the saliva beneath his tongue.

"What did she do?" he asked the owner.

The owner didn't answer. He just kept mopping up the blood, and when he had finished, he stepped over to the sink to rinse out the bar rag.

"What the hell did the woman do to deserve this?" Colter wanted to scream at the old man who used to be Mauldin, but instead kept his voice low and directed toward the Indian named Leroy standing next to him. "What the hell did this poor woman ever do?"

"What do you care, white man?" The Indian was looking at Colter directly. "Got nothing to do with you." There was no defiance in his eyes, nor anger, nor was there any anger in his face or manner of speaking at all. It was a sincere question. He seemed unable to imagine why a white man would even get involved. "We can take it from here, okay?"

"How long has this kind of shit been going on?" he asked the Indian.

The Indian just looked at him, still without smiling or frowning, without any expression at all in his face.

"Since long before you were born, white man. You wouldn't believe how long." Disgusting!

Chapter Twenty

Christ almighty, he had to get out of this place.

Outside it was still and very cold, and his mouth felt like it was stuffed full of an old sock. On the street there was no sign of the night-watchman's black pickup, Colter figuring he must have parked in the alley behind the bar. He walked across the street to the hotel. Out back, Leon was asleep in the cab. The whole town appeared asleep except for low strains of music, oddly mixing in the night air now from the two bars. Thinking to hear at least the sound of the black pickup, he heard nothing but the low throbbing of his own diesel. He thought about checking the end of the alley but had no idea what he would do if he found the truck or its owner.

The hotel sign that had made so much noise in the wind the night before was strangely silent, and Colter could hear above the idling of his truck the sound of his own footsteps going up the back stairs.

Back in the room, with the effects of the beer and the crashing aftermath of confrontation, Colter collapsed into a wingback chair near the window. He gazed out the front window of the hotel onto the silence of the snow, with the nightwatchman's black pickup now somehow angle parked just off the four-way stop, and in his dreams an Indian danced in the street. Falling snow blanketed the streets and the alleys and the whiteness of it lit the town at midnight as if it were dawn. In the light from the streetlights the snow fell slowly, gently, and into the quiet stillness of the silent intersection, beneath the suspended, blinking red light, the naked Indian danced. Slowly raising his bony knees to a silent, unheard rhythm, the Indian crouched and bucked, thrusting his torso with its long, flopping member first to the right, then to the left in a graceful pantomime, gradually stepping out a circle within the squared center of the four-way stop. The dance was all a slow bucking and bowing and a twisting to the side in the manner of a hunting beast, the Indian's head and shoulders defined by the pointed nose and erect ears of a wolf, a coyote. A dancing coyote with a horse's dick. Colter was transfixed by the scene, the coyote's hypnotic movements, and in his sleep he was strangely conscious of fending off danger, sensing that if he slept, then the terrible mythical being would surely steal upon him, compel him against his will to join in the dance. The hunt.

$\mathcal{C}$ Sunday, April 3, 1994

Chapter Twenty-one

Colter awoke slowly to a dull ache in his lower back, his neck stiff from trying to sleep in the chair. With his watch broken he had no idea of the time. Unable to shake the powerful reality of the dream even after a few moments of staring out the curtained window onto a deserted Main Street, he thought, what the hell, gather up the mutt and head for the farm. Wouldn't be the first time he'd slept warm and safe in the sleeper cab and it probably wouldn't be the last. Big bag of chips, half a dozen PayDays and Zero bars, TP, and a water bottle in the rations box. Just get out of town, avoid any more chance encounters with The Law, and spend the day at the farm looking around, maybe come to some decisions about it, then come back in on Monday for the trailer. Head on down the road. Get on with the rest of his life. And no matter how sorry his own life seemed, it sure beat the days and nights of those poor bastards hanging around Mauldin's.

Leon whined in protest at being awakened in the middle of the night, but within minutes Colter had thrown on clean clothes, loaded the cab, and to keep the throbbing sound of the diesel down, idled quietly out of town.

The nightwatchman's truck was nowhere in sight, but tire tracks through the newly fallen snow of the intersection headed west, making Colter wonder about the black truck in his dream. If they were the nightwatchman's tracks, he was probably headed for his security rounds out west toward a cluster of newer houses on the lake road. Colter turned north on spur 33, away from the tracks and toward the farm. After the trouble at the bar and then the total weirdness of the dream, he had looked forward to a little road time by himself, but leaving the scatter of streetlights behind and driving off into the empty countryside, Colter felt an odd sadness, as if he were departing a familiar harbor for open sea, leaving all of humanity behind on the thin, lighted shore slowly disappearing in his outside mirror.

He knew to take the second section mile line to the east. Wishing now he had made a reconnaissance during daylight, he was not sure which northbound dirt track led to the farm. Thirty years was a long time. Nothing in the snowy landscape looked even vaguely familiar along the first one, so he backtracked, bootlegging the tractor unit around at a pasture gate, and headed east again, searching for some landmark in the monotony of deserted fields. Knowing the creek would eventually come in from his left, he watched closely for the railroad crossing, and beyond the crossing, the old WPA bridge, remembering suddenly, and for no reason he could imagine, the swallow nests that lined the arch on the upstream side. For once he was in no hurry to get anywhere, and with the dirt roads frozen solid beneath a windswept layer of snow, Colter gave hardly a thought to getting the rig stuck.

Bootlegging the rig around at the second pasture gate, Colter was startled when his headlights brushed across a dried coyote carcass hanging stiff and desolate off a fence post, its thin fur lifting in the night wind. The jarring image was gone in a second, and knowing the length of the tractor and the narrow track of the road, he was able to keep the drive duals up on the crown and out of the barrow ditch. After the second turnaround Colter was certain he could go anywhere on the frozen roads. Within minutes, he pulled in at a familiar turn into the pasture high on the east side of the home place, crunching confidently through a drift behind the open wire gate, and shut the lights down, leaving the engine at low idle.

The farm lay midway along a rise of ground to the north of town.

The upper pasture along the east side pushed against the abandoned tracks of the Doodlebug, a 1940s milk run and passenger spur off the old Atchison, Topeka & Santa Fe mainline, then fell gently away to the west. The hillside gave a view back toward town, with its scatter of distant lights diminished beneath a vast and starry night sky, but beyond the windshield the snow lay beneath the starlight like a dusky blanket in a wide draw of the creek.

Leon lay still for a moment, taking in the unusual silence and dark and the cold night air coming in the open window, then stretched and looked over to Colter for his expected routine assistance.

The wind blew through the night, whistling above the chrome exhaust stack and rocking the cab ever so slightly in the strongest gusts. As always, Colter left the driver-side window open. The air seemed so enchanting and clean that when he awoke for his nightly pee he climbed all the way down out of the cab to look at the stars instead of using the nightjar. Colter had not noticed the stars for years, distracted nightly by the endless stream of headlights, the lighted truck parks, the exhausted sleep of the dead while on the road, so nothing had prepared him for the expanse of night sky, the spread of the Milky Way, stretched like a gauze veil from horizon to horizon. My God, he thought, caught up in a moment of childlike awe, who could count them? And what was it old Myrtle had said, something about going off on a star path? He wondered if this was what she meant. Well past what he figured was the middle of his own life, the stars simply looked cold, indifferent, devoid of any meaning beyond their indescribable beauty.

Leon never stirred, but with a faint gathering of light in the east a little after five, Colter awoke again, and this time Leon was ready. Colter awoke hungry, too, but the pull of the air and light, the empty countryside at his feet proved too much, and he decided immediately on a brisk morning walk, popping a stick of Juicy Fruit for breakfast.

The farm fell away to the west, down a gentle slope of new wheat the tenant farmer had planted carefully in thin rows that followed the contour of the hill. In the dawn light the thin lines of green suggested the tracings of a topographic map, each gentle swell of the land marked with a smooth turning of the lines. He remembered chopping the maverick cedars off this very hillside pasture when he was a boy. His father had dropped him off one Saturday armed with a Boy Scout hatchet and a file, and Colter's job had been to crisscross the pasture and lay to waste all the bright green new Christmas trees that invariably sprung up from the parent cedars along the creek. He had walked back and forth across the hillside a time or two, then lay back on the spongy turf of pasture grass and watched the airborne specks of turkey vultures wing thin black circles against a backdrop of white cloud. He listened for a long time to the noisy clatter of crows in the cottonwoods along the creek, and by evening, when his father returned, he had hardly made a dent in the crop of new cedars. His father had to hire an Indian to finish the job, another in a long list of disappointments.

Underfoot the reddish soil was frozen solid between the rows of wheat, so that none of it clung to his Nikes. Off to the left lay the rounded clump of sandhill plums, taking up maybe an acre or two toward the top of the hill. He remembered what Oliver had said about the nightwatchman digging around in the old Indian graves and thought briefly about a halfhearted investigation, but the pull of gravity led him toward the valley and the gentle blanket of drifted snow along the little creek. The stream cut appeared black against the light blue of the snow, the dark cedars standing out like sentinels against the background of winter-bare cottonwood and elm in the predawn light. Colter had always liked the way the tree branches made rounded shapes along the creeks in winter, like sleeping bears. In the growing light he was drawn toward the largest of the shapes, a rounded grove of chinaberry that clung to the far side of the little stream just below the ruins of the old homestead.

The house, like nearly everything else from his childhood, was gone now. Colter could see the barest line of blackened foundation stones beyond the leaning barn. Down the hill, through the branches of the bare chinaberry trees, he could just make out the dome shape of the old brick springhouse and root cellar. Partially hidden by a winterkill of overgrown devil's-claws and creeping gourd vines, the darkened cellar entrance drew his eye, an unchanged marker he hadn't visited in half a century.

He remembered summer days playing with Oliver and Johnny

along the creek below his grandfather's old house. The cellar was down the hill far enough to be out of sight of any grown-ups who might have had business with the barn or any of the working pens. Fenced out to protect the spring from livestock, always cool in the damp shade of the chinaberry trees where the spring seep made the ground wet all summer, the cellar offered a remembered haven from that relentless hot south wind that burned the edges of Colter's prairie childhood. The old fence was down now, strands of rusted wire hanging loosely from a half dozen rotted posts, and beyond lay the gaping dark of the cellar door.

Colter made for it through the snow.

Chapter Twenty-two

Hidden in the tangle of dried gourd vines and devil's-claws, the capped brick air shaft and an arched section of exposed brick above the dark hole of the doorway were all that showed of the old springhouse. The sight produced a moment of longing, but like most of the familiar sights of the day before, for what, exactly, Colter couldn't say. The Way Things Were, he guessed. He took his hands out of his jacket pockets and bent over to gather a little snow, anticipating the touch and feel of it against his skin. Leon was bounding ahead like a puppy into the soft drifts when something zipped overhead, the whizzing sound joined instantly to the nearby and unmistakable clap of a gunshot.

"Hey," Colter yelled out, ducking to one knee.

Instantly calculating the distance across the drifted snow to the shelter of the springhouse, Colter froze, stopped short by the warning bells of that old demon, claustrophobia. His first thought was of a stray shot from some hunter unable to see clearly into the tangled creek bottom in the half light of dawn. He called out again, but Leon had already freaked, bounding away through the deep snow toward the hillside and the open barn door a hundred yards or so uphill from the spring. The second shot whacked into Leon's chest, lifting him off his feet with a piercing squeal and dropping him stone dead onto his own tracks, and Colter knew. In the same instant he knew Leon was already beyond help, Colter stumbled forward into an awkward crouching run toward the cellar doorway, waiting each second for an imagined white light when the round would strike the side of his head, hoping against all logic that it wouldn't hurt.

Snow had drifted into the opening, disguising the shallow steps leading down into the darkened cellar. Missing his footing on the first one, Colter plunged headlong into the shadowed interior. As he tumbled onto the frozen floor he felt a burning in his left palm, sensing the litter of old broken canning jars and cursing at once the enduring nature of glass. Back on the fucking edge. Again. And at my age, he thought, wanting more than anything to cry while he gathered himself to his knees and gingerly removed a shard of broken glass from the bloody palm of his left hand. Won't Marilyn be pleased, he thought, then all he could see was Leon lifting miraculously from the ground, his shape contorted as if he had encountered some invisible force field, then sprawling onto the drifted snow, his short leap and fall somehow distinct from the sounds of the second round, from his terrible squeal of surprise and pain. Colter imagined slicing across the fat man's throat with a box cutter and watching the monster's eyes roll back while he bled out. In the sudden flood of rage Colter nearly, but not quite, forgot his predicament.

Trapped like a rabbit in a hole, he suddenly thought how ducking into the cellar opening might be the last dumb thing he ever did.

The old cellar door at the base of the steps had long ago fallen loose from its top hinge and leaned at an angle from the frame beside the opening. Colter knew at once that he was going to have to change his mind and run for it now, right now, or swing the door closed to avoid becoming an easy target when the nightwatchman came down to finish his kill. Running back out into the open might have worked except the bastard had a clear field of fire for at least thirty yards beyond the cellar to the tree line, and inside that thirty yards he could probably nail anything that moved. The words "hunting accident" came suddenly to mind. With the door blocked shut there was no way the sonofabitch could get at him except at close range. He couldn't wait up there on the hill forever, and if he did stumble his way down through the brush he probably wouldn't even fit through the cellar doorway. Colter longed for the comforting feel of the little .32 snug in the palm of his good right hand, but close enough quarters and the odds tipped back in his favor anyway. Wait it out until dark and the odds rose enormously. Problem was, Colter wasn't at all sure he could go on breathing with the door pulled to. Shutting it all the way seemed out of the question. Not yet anyway. At least not until he found a weapon. He took a deep breath, swallowed, and turned around to face the darkness.

Chapter Twenty-three

To the nightwatchman, observing now through the glasses, Tyree's truck cab, brown with spattered mud and parked just inside the east fence on the far hill, looks odd, incomplete without the trailer. The nightwatchman imagines Tyree lumbering the cab awkwardly across the tracks and over the cattle guard into the edge of the wheat field sometime in the night, and he thinks to himself how handy it would be to live out of a thing like that. Having endured years of furnished rooms, he appreciates the flexibility such a life might offer, and thinks to look into maybe picking up a cheap, used RV sometime soon.

For now, though, the nightwatchman puts the glasses aside and gently touches the raw scratch along the left side of his face. Too bad about last night. Serious miscalculation. Should have checked out the front first. Funny how things happen. Just when you think you know something cold, know your way around, you find out you don't know anything at all. Nothing. He would like to stay around long enough to settle things with Tyree in a little more personalized manner, but killing the dog helps. Now, with his things packed and ready to leave just in case, he knows he's doing the prudent thing. You can't just up and shoot a white man. Not and get away with it. Provoke him maybe, piss him off enough to get in the way of something "official." But still risky.

But doing them both in a hunting accident is another matter entirely. The Indian has been a royal pain in the rear for a long time now anyway. If something happens to them both, well, something bad is always happening around coloreds. Suicide, or cutting each other up on a Saturday night, or doing a little bad coke. Or the really desperate ones frying their brains on canned Sterno. Amazing. It's always one thing or another gets them. Then, too, a little hunting accident will forever teach the arrogant bastard not to run around the countryside looking like a mangy coyote. One rock, two shit birds. Bad things happen when you lose a war, he thinks to himself. Any war.

The man can't see clearly into the tight, rounded grove of winter-bare chinaberry trees near the cedars at the bottom of the hill, but from his vantage point inside the barn he can observe all lines of approach to the grove and the old brick cellar, and knowing the Indian's habits like he does, this is just as good.

The only other hint of movement had come a few moments after the second round took out the tan Lab, when three cottontails hopped cautiously out of the cedars to browse again on sprigs of pasture grass poking out of the deep snow along the creek. He had watched closely, even sighting in on the big buck until his eye caught the movement of a coyote trotting down across the far field on a beeline diagonally toward the rabbits. He shifted the rifle, laying up the front bead sight into the notch and swinging the barrel perhaps a yard ahead of the advancing coyote, then up a couple of yards to allow for the falling trajectory of a .30–30 round at that distance, and then he silently held the lead while the coyote closed on the rabbits. Just as the coyote paused to test the wind, turning his head to the side a little as if to gather sound as well as scent, the man squeezed gently on the cold metal trigger, ever so gently, until the sudden, always a little unexpected give and *click* of a dryfire. He thumbed back the hammer on the slim, light Marlin with a practiced smoothness, never losing for a second the exact lead the barrel bore down on the again advancing coyote. Just as the coyote was about to disappear into the cedars, the man squeezed the trigger again, producing the same dry *click* as before.

Then, at the precise moment the first rabbit bolted, the nightwatchman, smiling in the darkness at his own immense powers of life and death, carefully lifted the sighted rifle from the line of fire. Pivoting the rifle slowly with his left hand so that the barrel arched up toward his left shoulder, he had quietly moved the lever through another series of soft clicks, ejecting a second, still-warm, spent cartridge and chambering another round. The coyote, missing the rabbit in a split second of indecision, had stopped dead still in a clearing between the cedars. An easy target, but the nightwatchman, patient for bigger game, had waited.

Now, half an hour later, with Tyree pinned in the cellar and the low, cold sunlight slanting into the barn door and starting to glare a little off the drifted snow, he thinks it is nearly time for that crazy fucking Indian to appear.

Chapter Twenty-four

It is a perfect time for one of Oliver's usual dawn patrols. He feels the urge to be walking off across open ground, to feel the cold dawn breeze in his face, but after all that bullshit his dog soldiers reported at Mauldin's last night, and now this, he thinks he'll just follow along, ghostlike, and check on the prodigal son.

In less difficult times he might ambush his ass, maybe let him get a look at a real wild Indian. He wishes he could have found his hatchet. Jesus. Buried under the snow along with the rest of the woodpile. But a wild Indian with a coyote skin headdress and a tomahawk? Too bad this wild Indian had been in such a hurry to check on Tyree that he only had time to grab the headdress. Just the thought of the effect he can have with a minimum of props makes Oliver smile to himself. He wishes he could afford the time to go back to his Airstream and find all the necessary paraphernalia, but duty calls. He will have to settle for just following along quietly this morning. As Coyote, he'll tag along invisibly and keep his old friend Cole Tyree company from a distance. Maybe he can work in a third performance before Cole leaves town again. He knows down in his bones there should be another performance. He knows it. He thinks the first one in the alley behind the pool hall went well enough, but the second one, right in the middle of the deserted four-way stop at midnight, had been spectacular and clearly deserves an encore.

Oliver listens to the sound of the idling truck, and when certain he's alone, steps quietly around the Johnson grass and, moving smoothly into Cole's tracks, slides lightly down the snowy bank, careful as always to leave little sign of his passing. Solitary long-range sniper patrols years ago in the Nam have cured Oliver of any carelessness. Adventures, his crazy CO used to call them, just before the end. Mr. Clean in the woods, all right. Take nothing but long, clean shots, leave nothing but bones. Oliver had learned his trade early and well. There's a split second of cold in his stomach when Oliver remembers why he is truly here, but it passes quickly. He's sure that the fears of that old woman who hides in his heart are groundless. Cole's just out walking the old home place, Oliver thinks again. Been gone half a lifetime, and now he's just out poking around on his grandparents' old home place in the cold, snowy dawn. When he's satisfied there's nothing really left here for him, he'll go away again and never come back.

Oliver had watched three decades of boy scouts take the familiar route from town out along the creek on their qualifying five-mile hikes, listening to their chatter. During his rare R and R days in Thailand, Oliver had become very partial to the mellow sounds of the Grateful Dead, and during the noise and despair of the seventies, home from the war and drunk or stoned most of the time, he had only been able to tolerate the boy scouts and the screeching of their portable radios because some blessed savior had invented the Walkman cassette player, which he wore with earphones. He had watched from the deep cover of the woods and silently trailed the scouts like the unseen Coyote he really was, and never once in all those years had anyone even come close to the old springhouse.

He knows the creek will spread out into a wide draw not too far ahead. It will soon be glaring brightly, with the open draw full of slanting dawn sunlight on snow, and he knows he can't risk getting much closer. He'll hang back a bit, until Cole has a chance to cross the open draw and enter the woods again. Folding his long, skinny frame like a carpenter's rule, he leans back against the feathery bark of an old cedar to wait.

And Oliver can wait. Boy, can he wait. It is his second consummate skill. Oliver has taken waiting to the level of a fine art over the last thirty-five years, but something about Cole's urgent tracks across the clearing makes Oliver uneasy.

Yes, indeed, this boy scout is headed somewhere, all right, and Oliver begins not to like the looks of it.

Still, there are a thousand places Cole could be headed. Probably the burned-out ruins of the old house. After all, it had been his grandparents' home. Freddie and Julian, those dog soldiers, thought they had overheard Cole talking trash at Mauldin's about camping out at the old place, but with this late spring storm putting everything back in the middle of winter, Cole surely meant camping in his sleeper rig. The truck still idled with a low growl just inside the northeast gate. Hoping that old woman worrywart down deep in his stomach is wrong, Oliver begins to wonder what in the world he would do if, after all these years, the owl coming for him at last turned out to be his old friend, Cole Tyree.

He can see the tracks, Cole's and the dog's, disappearing into the cedars on the far side of the open flood draw. He'll give Cole another five minutes just to make sure he isn't smart enough to wait inside the tree line and watch his back trail. Come to think of it, he knows next to nothing about Cole's wartime adventures. Have to remember to ask him about it. Oliver figures five minutes, tops, in this freezing cold. About the time it will take Cole to finish off that stick of gum. Oliver has already caught a whiff of Juicy Fruit on the still dawn air.

He is glad all over again he has worn the headdress. He gently strokes the soft, cold fur, another example of the bounty of death's sweet abundance. Oliver is very sensitive to the importance of the right outfit, and it is only with truly great reverence that he ever puts on the coyote headdress. He knows deep down that in the act of putting it on, he truly becomes Coyote. Oliver knows from the Nam that's how it works. He knows it from the ears of a dead VC tucked into that Saigon whore's stretched-out garter he wore as a helmet band to end out his tour. In the Nam he had been very careful to wear exactly the right thing every day, and he was sure it had brought him home. Then, too, he tends to think better with the headdress on. Some of his best thoughts have come since he started wearing it. Sooner would have been better, he thinks, but he lets that one go. Without the coyote eye sockets on top of his head that give him the second sight, and those ears, those sensitive little funnels into the wind, without the four hollow legs and the hardened paw pads flapping and tapping around his shoulders, and the tail flying out to the rhythm of the dance, Oliver often feels he is just another ex-drunk Indian about to be extinct. With the headdress on, Oliver sometimes has the very strong impression he might be an alien life form and immortal. Thinking this, he realizes he may have skipped another pill this morning.

Sure enough, after sprinting across the wide draw, low to the ground with quick starts and turns just as his friend Coyote has taught him, Oliver dances noiselessly into the tracks of his enemy, his prey, his friend. He follows Cole and the dog through a tangle of saltbush growing against the crumbling banks of the draw, and at the base of a snowy cedar he discovers the thin foil wrapper from another stick of Juicy Fruit.

Coyote would have to be careful here. He would have to be sly. Oliver is thankful again he has worn the headdress. That way he is practically invisible, and if Cole sees him, well, Cole Tyree will think nothing of seeing a coyote loping along out at the edge of his vision. And if he does react, well then Oliver will just dance away backward until Cole can no longer see him at all. He has used that trick more than once on the stupid nightwatchman, and he can certainly use it on a middle-aged, out-of-shape Cole Tyree. No problem.

Clearly the most Oliver can hope for this morning is that Cole won't go poking around the old cellar. He'll settle for that. Cole Tyree is probably the only other person alive, except for that obese nightwatchman, who even knows about the old cellar at the bottom of the hill. Everybody else is already dead.

Then, in quick succession, he hears two loud reports. Mixed in, all seeming to come to him in the same instant, is the sound of Cole shouting and the for sure and certain death wail of the dog. Oliver has heard it all before, this familiar, almost sickening sound of shit hitting the fan. When he hears it this time he knows The Time of the Great Unraveling is upon him, and his heart sinks all the way down to his balls.

Chapter Twenty-five

In the beginning all Colter could see was the vague outline of shelves along the right wall while he learned to breathe again. The air inside the cellar was dry and cold, incredibly cold, with none of the musty, damp smell of summer he remembered. As his eyes began adjusting to the dim light, he could make out the thinned ranks of broken, dusty canning jars still in place after nearly half a century. The floor was littered with an accumulation of mud and broken glass now frozen into a thin glacial sheet from the spring seep. From the winter cycle of freezing and thawing, the ice now nearly reached the doorway. The arched ceiling, festooned with cobwebs and tiny icicles that trailed down a thousand dangling rootlets, was much lower than Colter remembered. It rose in a close, curved reach of damp brick from just above the top shelf. Although he could see the shelves near the doorway, with their dusty rows of canning jars and spoiled preserves, they disappeared as he strained to see into the dim recesses at the back of the cellar.

Even as a child Colter had not liked playing inside the old spring-house, but he remembered from his reluctant underground adventures with Oliver and Johnny that there had been a niche, originally for a coal oil lantern, laid into the brick at the back wall below the air shaft. They had placed their candles there, the steady updraft of air from the damp cellar floor flaring the candlelight, making their shadows dance. There had been an old wooden table, too, and a metal folding chair, probably long since rusted to powder, but in the half light coming through the tangled veil of dried gourd vines and skeletal devil's-claw stalks shrouding the entrance, the back of the vault was lost in darkness.

Standing very still in the doorway, trying to adjust to the dim light, Colter could almost hear the laughter in his father's voice as he had told and retold the story of a tornado that had forced them all into this very place. It had happened when his father was a boy, and they all still lived on the farm. When the family emerged, frightened but unharmed, they found the storm had miraculously spared the farmhouse and hay barn but the cyclone had removed the calving shed from the face of the earth, and the only thing left of the chicken house was a mostly plucked and very humbled rooster. It was distinctly a young voice that Colter suddenly remembered, and in laughter it carried nothing of the harsh and demanding tones Colter had later learned to brace himself against. His father's voice had changed once more, too, near the end of the story. Colter remembered a slight quiver, a momentary loss of control as he told of the family huddled together, praying by the dim glow of a coal oil lamp, waiting to see what the Lord had left them of all they owned. In remembering, Colter began to imagine his father's fears, to grasp the impact of the man's difficult beginnings on the way he lived his life. Suddenly, from the perspective of his own stumbling journey, Colter began to see the old farmstead for what it must have finally become to his father: just a broken-down little dust bowl farm out in the sand hills where in summer and winter he had worked away his childhood. An embarrassment. A place to escape. Alone now, bleeding from a painful cut, afraid for his life and trapped like a frightened rabbit in the same hole, Colter could maybe understand now, for the first time in his life, why his father might have become who he was.

Colter didn't like the darkness at the back of the cellar, but he felt too exposed with his back to the open door and so turned again to face the light. His hand, which at first had simply stung, had begun to ache, but in the light he could see the cut across his palm was superficial.

His fingers were sticky with drying blood, and he could tell by gently clenching and unclenching his fist that no tendons had been cut. Luck of the Irish, he thought.

For a brief moment of indecision while he felt in his pocket for the comforting shape of the lighter, Colter again considered just bolting. Then, with the lighter safely in his good right hand, he listened for what seemed an eternity. Hearing absolutely nothing but the idling of his truck and the calling of a distant crow in all the wide, snowy valley, he took another breath and swung the door around on its single rusty hinge, shutting out the light.

Despite the years that had obviously passed since the door had hung properly, the fit was tight enough against the weathered door-jamb that Colter was unprepared for the abrupt and nearly solid blackness that enveloped him. It was the blackest black he could remember, like drowning in a pool of black ink, a black he had imagined, and avoided, his entire life. He wondered if this was what it had really been like over there, waiting in the dark jungle night for death to come. Wondered if he would ever be able to forgive himself for not going. At first the silence was as overwhelming as the darkness, and as absolute. The only sound he could immediately identify was the ringing in his own ears. Then something in the darkness moved, and Colter could hear the sounds of tiny rodent feet, first rustling through something dry, old newspaper perhaps, then tinkling lightly across shards of broken glass. He stopped breathing, and in the silent darkness the faint rustling sounds of the rodent magnified out of all proportion until they completely drowned out the ringing. He listened so hard he could hear his own heartbeat, stared so intently into the face of absolute darkness that his eyeballs began to ache, and reflex alone suddenly struck the little BIC to life.

When still very young, Colter had imagined horrifying moments inside this very same dark place while tornadoes raged overhead. He had imagined himself trapped and about to suffocate as the ceiling began to crumble and bury him alive, but when he turned again to examine the darkened interior in detail, nothing could have prepared him for the body that lay curled upon the old wooden table below the air shaft niche.

His first reaction was to fight back the bile coming into the back of his throat. Holding onto the faithful BIC lighter in his good right hand and torn between the demon horrors of darkness or light, Colter had to choke back his gag reflex with his bloody left hand to avoid making any more noise. He could feel the slippery blood against his lips, could smell the copper as strongly as if he were a child again, sucking on a penny. There was a second when Colter just thought about letting go. Just let it go. Just go away for a moment. Where, exactly, would not have mattered nearly as much as simply going there. Letting go. He guessed it was what you finally did when you died. He thought of the utter peacefulness embodied in the long, exhaled sound of his mother's last breath in the nursing home, imagined a contentment his father might have felt as the wracking shudders of his violent and final heartbeats began to subside. For what seemed an eternity while he gazed upon the human remains before him and concentrated on the racing of his own heartbeat, Colter savored the thought of simply letting go. Sweet Jesus, he thought, what are *You* doing here? It was Easter morning now, and Christ still lay dead in the tomb. And from the looks of things, He had been here far longer than the alleged three days. Colter stood stock-still, transfixed by the vision in the steady glow from the lighter flame, thinking, Jesus, if that isn't You, then where are You when I need You the most? The body, clothed in rags, lay on its side. Had it been propped up and looking at him from the folding chair, Colter figured his heart muscle would have simply stopped in midbeat.

The sightless skull, still housed in a thin helmet of tattered flesh, lay cushioned on what was left of a baseball cap, while the lower jaw, no longer solidly attached to the rest of the skull, had sagged like the cellar door and hung now by a sinew of dried skin. The knees were drawn up in death as if to fit comfortably atop the little wooden table that straddled the now-frozen seepage basin.

Colter knew he couldn't hold down on the flame trigger of the BIC forever. With wavering faith that the thing on the table couldn't possibly hurt him, and reconciled to collecting his thoughts while conserving lighter fuel, he backed against the door and let the cellar again go black. Later, much later, Colter could not have told how long he stood quietly in the dark.

Finally, allowing himself to breathe silently in and out, in and out, through his open mouth, he began to feel a spreading sense of calm. The fear had not left. Rather, he could feel its presence out there around him in the dark, like the thing on the table or the ancient webs hanging from the arched brick overhead. It was almost as if he could, for the first time in a very long time, objectively perceive his own terror. It was as if he stood beside it, and were it not for the blackness, could actually look upon it as a distinct entity, separate from himself, and reaching out, might touch it. He remembered the hours and minutes and seconds leading up to his first parachute jump in the Airborne School at Ft. Benning, remembered the very second, in fact, that separated all the weeks of fear and dread during training from the act itself. In that split second it took to exit the aircraft he had stood outside his own fear and acted. In that split second those many years ago, something inside him had died. And something else, something newer and cleaner and better, had been born. Colter felt suddenly energized in the remembering. He could feel himself centering again. Poised, Colter struck the trusty little BIC again, thinking, let there be light.

Chapter Twenty-six

With grim fascination Colter moved toward the body, the lighter held high beside his head. On the way he cast, like a wide net, a generic little prayer for all the people he had ever known who had died, starting with the girl at the river, and wondering how many of them looked just like this by now. The flame sizzled in the drooping cobwebs, but held high it illuminated as much of the cellar as possible. He walked carefully, trying not to slip on the thin skin of ice on the floor and repeat his graceful entrance. Broken glass lay everywhere, some loose from a recently collapsed shelf, some frozen solidly into the ice, but a half dozen halting steps brought him as close as he wanted to be to the body. It lay curled atop the old table with its back to the wall below the lamp niche, and Colter was about to take a closer look when a thin needle of daylight at the back of the niche caught his eye.

The lamp shelf was nearly a foot across and a brick and a half deep at the bottom and extended upward another three feet until it narrowed abruptly and disappeared as a vent shaft behind the arched ceiling. He could see that the narrow shelf contained three distinct items faintly backlit by the tiny sliver of light. Dead center, in the upturned lid from a canning jar, stood an unburned white plumber's candle with the little white wick still folded over into the wax. To the left sat a small black vinyl box, oblong and rounded at the ends as if it might contain a watch or a pair of glasses, and propped up on the right stood a shiny metal tube with some kind of curved wire stand at the bottom. Stepping closer, leaning gingerly above the shrunken body, Colter tried to examine the items without breathing and without letting anything of himself touch anything on the table. His thigh just brushed the forward edge and the whole thing swayed as if his very breath might collapse it. Something seemed odd about the arrangement, though, the items were too carefully placed, and then it dawned on Colter that there were no cobwebs in the niche at all. Cobwebs hung in great, dusty festoons from the edges of the ceiling. They draped like a thin lace veil from every remaining jar along each shelf and fell in matted nets in the dim corners and around the sides of the doorway, but there were no cobwebs at all in the niche or on any of the objects. Colter thought back to what Oliver had said about the nightwatchman digging up Indian graves. He flashed on the black market that might well exist in Cheyenne grave offerings, but the objects on the shelf were obviously not grave offerings, nor was this still-clothed body skeletal enough for some anonymous, excavated Cheyenne. The surprising cleanliness of the shelf was an obvious sign of recent attention, as if the niche were a kind of altar that someone regularly tended. He pried up the candlewick with a fingernail and lit the candle, nearly burning his thumb waiting for it to catch. Then he blew gently on the lighter to cool the jet and replaced it in his pocket.

In the steady shine from the candle flame Colter picked up the small black case. Inside was a crisp U.S. Army–issue Purple Heart and lying atop the attached ribbon, the tarnished crossed rifles of a sharpshooter's badge. Oliver. He knew immediately the medal and badge were both Oliver's, and he knew just as suddenly, knew without even looking down, that the skull before him on the table would be flattened slightly across the back from a little too long on the cradleboard. Johnny. Johnny Lonewolf.

On closer inspection there were spiderwebs on the body, too, and beneath the veil of webs, the tattered remnants of a T-shirt, a rotted pair of Levi's 501s. An honest-to-God pair of black-top Keds hung loosely on shrunken, skeletal feet. Over the years the canvas tops had shrunk and tightened until the toes of the tennis shoes now turned up like the shoes of Aladdin. A dark stain had spread across the table from the slow, relentless process of decomposition, but it was clear from the dry, thin stain that the process had taken place long ago. In the cold, dry air there was certainly no smell to associate with a decomposing body, nor was there any sign the body had ever been scavenged by any animal larger than an occasional rodent. Nor did it appear, given the fetal, almost comfortable position in which he lay, that Johnny had been moved at all following death. The shrinkage and drying were so evident it was hard to put a size to the body, but Johnny's position on the table almost suggested that he had simply folded up so as to fit as comfortably as possible on the table and died. The bullet hole was as small and neat as if it had been drilled into his left temple with a quarter-inch Black & Decker.

Hard to believe such a little hole could void so much life and time and potential. Because of that little hole, Johnny Lonewolf had skipped over the last forty years on fast-forward. To breathe, or not to breathe, that was sure as hell the right question. For the first time in his life, standing over the body of his onetime friend in a dark, cold hole in the ground, Colter knew he was going to die. No sliding by. No more Grace. No bullshit. Maybe not now, but maybe now, and he found his own calm acceptance of the notion strangely liberating.

Pocketing the medal box and its contents without a moment's thought, Colter glanced instead at the stainless steel tube propped up in the niche.

Chapter Twenty-seven

"It was an accident, Cole. I swear it."

The voice, calm and deliberate, came from just beyond the spring-house door, and the first scary thing was that Colter hadn't heard anyone coming at all. Not a sound. Preoccupied with examining what he assumed was a murder weapon, he had not heard so much as a footfall, not the rustle of a single weed stalk outside the door. "Accident" was suddenly a comforting possibility.

The second scary thing, accident or not, was that Oliver had obviously invested a great deal of energy over a long period of time in hiding whatever had happened here. Colter could well imagine the enormity of the effort, the self-mastery involved in managing the fear of discovery. Although he had certainly never killed anyone, he often suffered through dreams in which he *had* killed. The reasons were never that important, dissolving like mist in the morning light. What lingered was that bizarre, nightmarish struggle to avoid detection, to bury the body where no one would ever find it. He had read once, in some pop psychology article in a stack of waiting room magazines, that the dream, common to many, had to do with his own frustrated efforts at uncovering a buried part of himself. Unresolved issues about growth and change, or some such New Age bullshit. It was the kind of self-analysis he found too tedious to contemplate, but he remembered the palm-sweating fear that always accompanied the dream. Given his own early horror story, and what lay behind him now on the table, he could well imagine the slow erosion of a soul beneath the weight of a lifetime of such deception.

Now, like that Greek guy who blinded himself, Colter suddenly knew much more than he had any business knowing. Figuring the burden of knowledge might soon weigh heavily, he stood stock-still, backlit by the plumber's candle, his shadow huge and black against the doorway, and fingered the single .22 hollow-point round he had just extracted from the little gun.

"You the shooter this morning?" Colter asked quietly.

Under the cover of his own voice, he carefully replaced the round where he had found it, positioning the flat cartridge base snugly against the spring-loaded hammer and pin at the business end of the steel tube with the faintest of clicks.

"I wouldn't have missed."

"Nobody missed," Colter said, seeing again the old retriever falling straight down, as if sliding down an invisible wall.

He tried to rethink his image of the nightwatchman, the imagined crosshairs trained on that reach of open ground where Leon now lay cooling in the snow. Stepping quietly to one side, closer to the rotting shelves, he pictured Oliver instead, standing in the landing just beyond the sunken doorway, rifle in hand, his breath making a fog in the early sunlight. The nightwatchman would have thought him unarmed. Oliver would know better.

"I heard two shots, Cole. You're still moving. Trust me, he missed."

Interesting word, "trust," Colter thought. "I bent over to touch the snow," he said, marveling again at the aura of Grace that seemed to surround him, hoping it was still intact. Then, "Why doesn't he take you out?"

"Can't see me. Shots came from the barn, right?"

"I couldn't tell. That's where Leon was headed, though," Colter said, seeing that picture again in his head. Trying to place the darkened barn door into it. Another silence, then, "What now, Crazy Horse, knowing what I know?"

"Your call, Cole. I was hoping to steer you away from here. Too late now. Easter Sunday, colder than a witch's tit out here, and there isn't any rescue party just over the hill. I'm it. He comes down the hill and shoots you like a skunk in a hole, I'm found out anyway."

"Got a plan?"

"We stay, he'll kill us both and report a hunting accident. Underbrush is too wet and cold to get a good SOS brushfire going. We got to get to a phone. Or a CB."

"Sorry. Kept meaning to get the thing fixed. And what about Johnny?"

"Johnny's been here for a long time, Cole. He doesn't have anywhere else to go. He was my brother, and a long time ago I accidentally killed him. And now I'm tired. Bone tired. I've never been so tired in my whole fucking life as right now."

Colter thought he could hear the tone and cadence of truth in the resigned voice outside the door. He wanted very much to hear it. "You armed?" he asked at last.

"That's my suicide round in that little toy gun you've probably got leveled at the door," Oliver said. "Don't waste it."

Chapter Twenty-eight

First came the blinding glare of low dawn sunlight after the cellar's darkness, with the knuckles of his right hand white from gripping the little tube gun. Then, in the three or four seconds it took them to skirt the left edge of open ground in front of the springhouse doorway, Colter was too busy waiting for the flash of whiter light that meant he was dead to even think about the coyote headdress. Nor, with his panting, out-of-shape version of the quarterback sneak, did he give it much thought for the first ten yards or so of noisy bushwhacking into the tangled second-growth willow.

Finally, though, crouched in the snow behind a flimsy blind of scrub willow while his breath began to come in ever-longer wheezes, Colter realized he might not have been dreaming last night in the hotel, that he might actually have seen this apparition before, dancing in the snow in its birthday suit. And now, in the distance, church bells. Jesus. Even if he lived to tell about it, Marilyn was never going to believe any of this. Not one word.

"The fuck is that on your head?" Colter whispered, staring into the empty eye socket and the upper half of a coyote face. The thing rode high on Oliver's head, with dangling little feet that settled lightly on his shoulders and a chinstrap that looked a lot like a bootlace. "This what that jackass was talking about in the diner?"

Oliver ignored him, looking instead out through the thin lace of willow stalks toward the barn. "Maybe he's gone," he said.

"You were obviously out and about. You see his truck anywhere?"

"Gate's been chained for months where the driveway turns in off the section line over west. If he parked at the gate, and he had to because he's too fat to walk a hundred yards, we couldn't see it from here anyway. Might not even hear him drive off."

"Shit."

"Yup. No way of knowing."

"How'd you get here?"

"Walked. I always walk. I'm the only Indian in the world without a pickup truck or an old Buick. Don't even have a relative owns one."

Colter looked again at the dyed black hair poking out around the coyote headdress, the Levi's jacket way too thin for this weather. "Think he saw us?" Colter asked, daring to speak above a whisper.

"Hard to tell. From the barn you can't see the cellar door. If you know what you're looking for you can see the air shaft, though, that little trace of red brick. If you know right where to look, and that's only now, in winter. But he uses binoculars."

Colter looked at him, listening.

"We were pretty low there to the left. He might not have seen us, but I guarantee he heard us. You anyway."

Colter thought about that for a moment. Then he thought about something else. "What happened?"

Oliver didn't move, his stare focused on the black hole of the barn door.

"You said it was an accident. I believe you. I wanted to believe you so that I could come out of there, and obviously I want to believe you now for other reasons. But how did you accidentally shoot Johnny in the left temple? Christ. I saw the hole."

"So stupid. So fucking stupid. And all those miserable years."

For the first time Oliver turned and looked at Colter directly, his eyes two gray, bottomless pools of sadness. Now, up close, Colter could see freckles, the lines around the eyes, the harsh verticals down from the corners of his mouth, and it was as if the clown's face Colter remembered from the diner, remembered even from childhood, had sagged into this wooden mask of grief beneath a scruffy coyote skin. It was cold lying in the snow in the shaded depths of a willow tunnel. Colter could see their breath mingling, could see the slight quiver of Oliver's shoulder shivering in the frozen air.

"How?"

"I wanted to carry the damn gun. That's all. Can you believe it? That silly little piece of crap you've got in such a death grip," he said, nodding at the gun. "I just wanted to shoot the damn thing, and he wouldn't let me."

"So you fought?"

"No, nothing like that. It wasn't that at all. I just tried to grab it on the run, like a joke, you know. Whack him upside the head, count a little coup when he crawled through the fence. Like I was always doing. Asshole held on. Bang."

"At the cellar?" Colter asked.

"Yeah. Right over there." He nodded toward the tan and crimson blemish on the snow that used to be Leon. "Faked him out a couple of times along the tracks until he dropped his guard. So fucking stupid. We got through the right-of-way fence, and it would have been my turn anyway once we got through the cellar fence. A hundred yards, I couldn't wait. I was going to go for help, but then he just died. Just like that. One minute we were laughing, kidding around, next minute he's on the ground looking up real surprised, and then he's stone dead with his eyes still open. I've been looking into that face ever since. Johnny and I got old the same day. Everybody talks about how going into the military matures you, makes you grow up. Bullshit. Fucking war made me a kid again. Every time I killed one of those little gook motherfuckers, I saw Johnny's face. Couldn't stop killing 'em."

Colter waited.

"Until the last one," he said. "I couldn't kill the last one. Any points for that one, Cole?"

"Yeah," Colter said. "You get extra points for that one."

"I didn't know what to do. I sat right down in the dirt beside him and cried my eyes out. Then I thought, shit, who'd believe me, us always fighting around at school. So I hid him. Laid him out on that old table thinking he might even wake up, but after that, I couldn't touch him again." Oliver looked away again. "I watched over him, though. Watched him change. Sweet sixteen, going on sixty now. Told everybody he ran off and joined the navy, and stuck to my story. It broke old Myrtle's heart, but that would have happened either way. I kept thinking somebody would find him, find me out. Call me home from that awful fucking place. Nobody ever did."

Colter had no idea what to say so he said nothing, fogging the cold air with his slightly wheezing breath and trying to remember what he might have been doing at the same time it was all going on. He remembered them asking at school about Johnny, but after a day or two it was old news. Must have been hell, he thought. Sure enough made him crazy as a bedbug, that dried-up coyote for a hat. But at least nobody's shooting now. At least that. He clenched his fist tightly around the breech of the tube gun.

They waited half an hour, hunkered down behind the screen of willow, their knees, elbows pushing through the snow into the frozen sand of the creek bank while they halved Colter's last stick of Juicy Fruit. Whispered back and forth about the past as if it could make any difference and waited for any hint the nightwatchman was still around. There had been no more shots, no movement, no sound at all from the narrow opening of the barn door. Colter was cold through to the bone and soaking wet from lying on the snow. He knew if he waited any longer it might take a crane to lift him, so he finally said, "Fuck it" and raised up on one knee to see a little wider about. Dawn air moved with a dry rustle through the last clinging leaves on the cottonwood overhead. Somewhere, could have been miles away in the stillness, a dog barked and Colter peered through the willow screen at Leon lying a few yards away in a slowly cooling heap. The morning sun, low at their backs now, shone golden on his tan, bloodstained coat in the clearing between the willow screen and the springhouse. Nothing moved but the last of the clinging leaves. Down the valley, toward the bridge and town, he could hear the clatter of distant crows, and from across the valley behind them came the rough, coughing sound of his tractor rig, idling faithfully as a trusty steed. Colter knew without even looking that they couldn't risk a break across the open wheat field to the truck without knowing for certain the bastard was gone. Keeping to the cover of the streambed, they might make it back to town and help. My kingdom for an armored personnel carrier, he thought.

They had been talking in low tones, agreeing that so far the night-watchman had done nothing he couldn't explain away as an accident. Even shooting Leon, for chrissake, with the dog's color so like that of a coyote. So he coaxed Oliver up into the lead and they headed downstream single file, away from the springhouse and toward the old WPA bridge and town, Colter feeling safe for the moment just following along behind the swishing coyote tail through a low, thin cover of willow and alder. The round came with the whisper of a baseball bat through the fleshy outside of Colter's upper left arm, tearing out muscle tissue and clipping the bone on its way into Oliver, knocking him to the ground before the real sound came.

When it came it came with a distant *crack*, as if from far, far away, as if the searing pain, the tearing of the flesh were an isolated phenomenon, unconnected to anything else in the universe. Lightning must feel like this, Colter thought in the split second before the second wave of pain hit.

Chapter Twenty-nine

Oliver was down on his right side, his eyes wide open, his mouth open, too, but no sound came. And then he squeezed his eyes shut, trying to push himself up again with his left arm, trying to take the weight off his pinned right arm, *dreaming the sound again, the little* POP *too faint a sound to matter. Such a little sound, coming from far away at the end of his arm.* The snow about them lay spattered with blood in a pattern of fine droplets radiating out from where Colter found himself stumbling to stay upright. He had spun a quarter turn to the right and wasn't sure he hadn't been unconscious for a second or two.

"Fuck," he said. "I'm shot, aaaaahhhhhhhh," feeling the odd warmth of his own blood sprayed onto his face from the exit wound. He couldn't move his left arm correctly or even unclamp his left fist. All the feeling was gone, as if the top of his left side had gone away, although all the pieces were right there for anyone to see. Except for the growing panic, numbness was way better than that first jolt of pain. Oliver was still trying to close his mouth. Finally, clamping it shut, he bared his teeth in a grimace, drawing his knees up toward his chest in a fetal hug, then rolled his head over and vomited. He lay on his right side, his coyote headdress still on but tilted into the soft, red-stained snow, his right arm still pinned, left elbow splayed up at an odd angle.

Colter thought he looked just like a photograph in one of his World Book Encyclopedias, couldn't think which one, some dead Indian lying frozen stiff in the snow after a famous battle. Old guy had one arm up in the air, frozen in place like he might have been waving it when he died, but other than that he looked exactly like Oliver. And Oliver suddenly looked a lot like Johnny.

"You in the club *now*, motherfucker," Oliver finally managed to say through clenched teeth. "What now, white man? You just gonna stand there?"

For a minute Colter couldn't think of an answer through the roaring of the pain. Then, between two waves, he said, "How the fuck do I know. I never did this before. Jesus. Wait for the cavalry?"

"That's funny," Oliver said. "That's really funny. Joke. What's the last thing an Indian sees before he goes to the happy hunting ground?"

"What?"

"The fucking cavalry AAAAAHHHHHHH," said Oliver, "my second time sweet Jesus that hurts but not like it's going to Christ they ought to have civilian Purple Hearts aaaahhhhh."

"This gets worse?" Colter had gone back to one knee, his left arm and shoulder hanging limp at his side, the handkerchief-wrapped left palm forgotten for the moment. He was trying to control the growing pain in his shoulder with his mind, and it was not working at all.

"That claymore blew, I had to wait an hour for a medic to get to me with morphine," said Oliver. "All that time slugging it out with the heat and the bugs and the smell of shit that wouldn't leave, motherfuckers dying all around you, and that was still only the second longest hour of my life," *and he could remember the quiet afterward, how the birdsong stilled for a moment then began again, that twittering chatter of sparrows in the chinaberry leaves, here it was fall and the birds noisy as springtime, as if nothing bad had happened, nor any soul just departed this earth.*

"The longest?"

"Back where that dog's lying. Within five, ten foot of that very spot."

"Where you hit?"

"Just be still and shut up for a second, okay? Just shut up now, Cole. I got to gather it all together. And get fucking down before he takes your head off. Aaaaahhh."

"The bullet is still in you. Christ. It went right through me and into you and it never came out. Fucking bullet is in there right now oh god oh god . . ."

"Get the fuck DOWN," Oliver hissed.

Colter dropped to his other knee, knowing if he went all the way down into the snow it would all be over anyway because he would never, ever be able to get all one hundred and ninety-three pounds up again.

The sun was well up now, flooding in above his idling truck at the top of the hill and turning the snow-covered ground a soft blue in the shadows against a bright orange wherever the sunlight fell. A beautiful, glorious morning, Colter thought, trying to move very carefully against the pain pounding back into his left arm. Without doubt, one of the most memorable Easter Sundays on record. Jesus. The fields about them had blown mostly clear of snow with two days of fierce north winds and now lay soft and unseasonably green, but the creek bottom, which afforded their only cover, lay deeply drifted in places. The creek was like a black snake winding in and out of the drifts so that you would never know for certain where the solid sandbank actually lay. The bottom widened out here near the old springhouse, a level floodplain with scattered creek elm and willow and very little cover with the sodden cattails all laid over and tangled into drifts of snow. The iron cold had frozen the surface of the creek, but beneath the film of ice the water ran cold and swift, making a useless little serpentine path. The flat floodplain was out of the question, too. Too open, a perfect field of fire from any of the surrounding hills.

"Now I'm a coyote," Oliver said, trying to reposition the headdress firmly on his head with his left hand. "I'm going to disappear. No problem." His useless right hand and arm lay pinned beneath him in the snow, the blood starting to soak through the lower right side of the thin Levi's jacket.

Colter stuffed a wad of soiled handkerchief into the ragged opening in front of his shoulder where the bullet came out, trying to stop the flow, but the wadded cloth quickly bled through. He used a loop of cast-off baling wire sticking up out of the snow to secure his arm to a belt loop, then tried to check out Oliver's back.

"Now," Oliver said, trying to adjust the headdress just so. "The sonofabitch can't shoot what he can't see."

"You got another one of those stowed away somewhere?" By lifting up the Levi's jacket Colter could see that there was truly no exit wound. The round had gone in clean, the hole pumping blood through the white T-shirt and onto the jacket. No way to tell what might be going on inside. From where it went in, Colter figured kidney damage, minimum. The blood was seeping slowly onto Oliver's lower back on his right side. Colter pulled the light jacket back down carefully over the wound.

He then clumsily tried to shift the little gun to his right hand. Easier said than done to pry the cold, dead fingers of his already damaged left hand loose enough to transfer the weapon. Good thing I'm a right-hander, he thought, imagining the most he could do anyway would be to swat somebody with the barrel. If they got close enough. He couldn't believe the bastard had his little .32, then wondered idly if he just might have it on him. He'd show the sonofabitch a thing or two if he had that little piece. Shove it up his ass and squeeze off a round. Fuck that. A clip. The little tube gun was another thing altogether. He hadn't had time to examine the breech action in the dark of the cellar, but when Oliver had spoken just outside the door he had immediately pulled the little round hammer knob into firing position. Now, clumsy as a hippo with only his right hand available, he cocked the hammer back all the way, eased back on the trigger, and closed the hammer slowly down onto the round into safety position.

"You think this round is still any good?" he asked.

"I been banking on it for some time now," Oliver said.

"Can you walk?"

"Can try. I'm thinking you slowed the round down a bit, but it still tore up something inside. Gonna need some attention before long. You know, if the crows come, we're dead."

Colter looked at him. "He knows within a hundred yards of where we are anyway. What's the difference?"

"Hollow points."

"That what went through us? Jesus."

"No, man. What we got was hard-nosed. That's the only reason you're still standing. From now on what we get is hollow point. You know, soft tip, spreads on impact. At muzzle velocity a round would probably spread going through a pat of soft butter. Some bad shit when they come out the other side, man. Spread your head like JFK's."

"Jesus. So what we don't want just now are crows. Gotcha."

"I feed 'em on my walks sometimes. Lots of times, actually. Nearly always. Corn," Oliver said. "I feed 'em corn."

"Got any corn with you now?"

"Sure." With his left hand he pulled out a handful of yellow kernels from his jacket pocket. "They're smart, though. Got to hope there's one finds it. He'll tell the others."

This is turning into a horse race, Colter thought. Two lame in a field of three.

With more than a little help, Oliver made it to his feet, and they pushed their way farther into the willows, leaving the yellow scatter of grain visible on the snow to draw the crows away. They tried then to stay low in the creek channel, stumbling through the drifts as quietly as possible, the creek looping beneath the sparse cover of the bare winter trees.

"He's going to hunt us like he would a wounded coyote," said Oliver. "He'll run us to ground in this sorry-ass sandy little creek bottom then circle around for a clean shot again. Goddamn Indians never did have any luck along these little creeks. Battle of the Washita. Fucking Sand Creek. Like I said, cavalry's probably waiting at that old cement bridge."

"Well, long as you wear that headdress he can probably claim hunting accident and get away with it," Colter said. "You look like a fucking coyote."

"I am a fucking coyote," Oliver said, stumbling into a drift and sliding down the steep bank into the thin skin of ice that covered the moving water. The ice gave way immediately while he struggled and cursed and clawed his way onto the snowy bank.

"Some coyote," Colter said. "I can sure see your ass. And hear you, too. Old Myrtle said you were crazy. Said you needed help. Boy was she ever right."

"Well, the sonofabitch didn't kill me, now did he?"

"It's still early."

They were only a few hundred yards down the creek when they heard the sound of an engine start up.

"Maybe he'll just go on down to the bridge, that little one over by Wheeler Snyder's old place, and try to ambush us there," Colter said. "He can't be that stupid. Can he? Somebody could come along."

"He's hunting now. He won't stop."

"He's not hunting. He's crazy."

"He's hunting. After the first one, the one that makes you puke, all the rest are just hunting. The best hunting there is. Nobody talks about it, but the hunting is what you miss."

"Jesus."

"You white eyes always talk too much," Oliver whispered. "Just shut up and listen for a minute."

The morning was still, church bells silent now in the full flood of morning light, and in the wooded bottom not a breath of air stirred. The sound of the truck was steady, like the driver was perfectly willing to let the engine warm up properly on this cold morning. Like he was in no hurry at all, taking his time, out enjoying an early morning coyote hunt. Most reasonable thing in the world, thought Colter. And then the sound changed as the driver eased the truck into motion and crept his way in low gear out onto sure ground.

"Fucker's coming after us. In the truck. Jesus."

They couldn't see up beyond the creek to the old house and the hill above where the black Toyota was parked, but the sound came from that direction. Then the truck stopped.

"Shut up," Oliver said, touching him on the shoulder. "At least right this moment he doesn't know exactly where we are. I'd like to keep it that way if possible. At least for a couple more minutes. At least until I can make my peace with the universe. And anyway, there's no road down here. Damn noisy honky. Christ this hurts."

Then the irregular idling of Colter's diesel, a comforting background noise, ended with a sudden sputter and cough.

"Your truck quit."

Observant sonofabitch. "Out of fuel in number one. Nobody to switch over. I sure never planned to be away from the cab this long."

"Hills on each side of the creek all the way into town, shoot, he can sit anywhere he wants along the high ground with a pair of field glasses and make sure we stay in the bottom here. No place to go but toward the damn bridge. What he's doing, he's herding us. Like a couple of dumb milk cows."

"Coyotes."

"Yeah. Coyotes," Oliver said. "He hunts this creek all the time. Nobody gonna think twice, seeing him up there banging away at the brush."

From far away back upstream, up beyond the springhouse where the creek was just a dry wash cut down through an upland pasture, Colter could hear the raucous call of a crow. Then just overhead three black crows cawed back loudly, headed upstream to join the party. Our one chance is to make it to the bridge before that bastard does, he thought. If there were a farmhouse, a busy highway, anyplace they could get to. There was nothing. Most of the old farmhouses were abandoned in the fifty-year migration to town. If they tried to hide out in the bottom until they could attract someone's attention, they'd bleed to death or freeze. Either way, strike one. In drier weather they might have fired the underbrush, brought help that way. Nothing would burn now with a blowtorch under it, and the first hint of smoke would bring a round or two of incoming. Strike two. Colter knew they had to get to the bridge to get any help at all, and it looked like Tubby was going to be at the bridge waiting. Their only hope would be that someone would come along right when they got there, otherwise strike three, we're out. Colter was still thinking about strike three when Oliver slipped again in the snow.

"Doing okay, Bud?" he asked, helping Oliver up by his jacket collar and his good arm.

"Getting a little light in the head's all," *and then far ahead, high up on the side of the valley and, at this distance, barely visible in the shimmering heat, he could see the loading chute and the old working pens, gray with age, and disuse. More than once they had climbed the windmill, braving the spinning blades for a hawk's view of the wide valley. Now the ancient, tin-blade Aeromaster, wired into mute submission with a twist of baling wire, stood silent, distant sentry above a rusted-out metal stock tank. The barn, sagging a little in the middle from a cracked ridgepole and weathered silver-gray in the morning sunlight, leaned away from the south wind coming through the sunflowers at the exact same angle as the dying windbreak elms beside the abandoned two-story house on the crown of the hill just beyond.*

They knew the ruins well. Once, it seemed like a long time ago, they had harvested smooth, white pigeon eggs from the hayloft in the barn and that same day had scrawled their names in soft charcoal on the rose-patterned wallpaper in the downstairs parlor of the old house.

"Don't die on me now," Colter said, trying to haul Oliver back to his feet again. "You can't die on me. Told me so yourself, so get a grip."

"Never said I couldn't wish for it."

"Nope," said Colter, trying to keep him talking. "You didn't. Wishing for it now?"

"Soon, Kimosabe. Soon." He was trying to walk, but the uneven ground, the icy footing in the steep creek channel, the drifts, the tumbled driftwood and vines and sometimes nearly impenetrable underbrush made the going tough.

"You're the woodsman, for chrissake." Urging him along.

"Don't know, man. Where I got blown up at least it was fucking warm. Everything feels blue, Cole. Am I blue?" He had stopped walking again and now stood perfectly still, looking at his left hand. "Is that sonofabitch blue, or what?"

"Red, man. You're a redskin, remember? You ain't blue," Colter said, lifting the Levi's jacket to examine the spreading stain. Removing the handkerchief gingerly from his own wound, Colter pushed the soaked cloth onto the seeping hole in Oliver's back, the wadded handkerchief soaked now clear through, their blood mingling, freezing in the open air of morning.

"We got to get the bridge behind us," said Colter. "No joke. Serious. Or we are going to die out here, man. You, anyway. And all the bastard has to do is keep us away from the bridge long enough."

"Thought I told you I couldn't die."

"Figuratively speaking, of course."

Oliver didn't say anything.

"What I mean is we've got to get you past the bridge. I'll live," said

Colter. "Round just took off a little fat, that's all. You could bleed to death inside. And I'm not kidding. I can't do anything about that."

Right now the issue was the bridge, and they had to be at least another quarter mile from it. If we could just stay out here and stay warm and not bleed to death, he thought. Then everything else would work itself out. The stupid beef run. Marilyn. The truck payment. Time heals all, he thought. Colter clung to that thought through another forty or fifty feet of snowbound struggle before his focus came back to the bridge.

"I asked you before, white man, but you never answered. What'd you do in the Nam, anyway?"

Colter took as deep a breath as he could and still stay inside the wall of pain. "You want to know something funny?" he said. "I never even went to Vietnam."

Oliver just looked at him. Smiled that toothless smile. "Knew all along I was fighting the white man's war for him."

"No shit. Went in the army, all right. Watonga draft board saw to that. Yanked my young self right out of carpentry school. Trade school didn't count the same as college. Already married, too, but the marriage deferment was long since gone up in smoke. Everybody else going, figured I'd be going too. So I volunteered. Signed up for OCS, Airborne, Rangers, Special Forces, shit, anything I could think of to make me some kind of badass. Going anyway, thought I might as well know what I was doing when I got there. Jesus. Twenty years old. Should have volunteered for clerk's school, for chrissake. Fastest ticket to the front."

"Wherever the fuck that was."

"Yeah. Well, with all the crap they taught me I'm still amazed they didn't ship me out to kill somebody. Somewhere. Ended up spending so much time in training units, my enlistment was up before I had time to go. Closest I got to combat was 1968, after the democratic convention in Chicago. Part of our unit in the 82nd got all decked out in starched fatigues, trousers bloused into those fine, spit-shined Cochran jump boots, and flew on up to Andrews in a C-141 Starlifter. Took a bus out to a staging area in some school parking lot across the Potomac from the Pentagon where we sat on our asses for half a day. Our mission, near as I could figure out later, was to protect the brains of the U.S. Army from Norman Mailer. Half the 320th Artillery Battalion, 82nd Airborne Division, versus a couple hundred flower children. Looking back, I figure it would have been about even. They never even issued live ammo. Can you believe that shit?

"Later on, Johnson's picking his dog up by its ears and sending twenty, maybe thirty thousand troops a month over there, I'm in fucking Alaska, learning to cross-country ski. Figuring somebody at the Pentagon must know something about the weather in southeast Asia they're not telling. Whole time, I never saw combat."

"Have now. Shot at's shot at. Don't make a shit who's shooting."

"Maybe."

"For what it's worth, your secret's gonna die with me shortly," Oliver said.

"Sooner than you think, you don't shut up," Colter said, trying to imagine someone, anyone coming to help.

Chapter Thirty

Afterward he couldn't have said when the idea began to form. Something to think about instead of thinking how cold his feet were in the wet Nikes. Quit trying so hard to get away and just kill the bastard. Hunter instead of hunted. Thinking back to something his dad had always said, that the best defense was a good offense. Thinking maybe it was why the old man was always out for a buck, that maybe having a little extra money on hand was not such a bad defense after all, never knowing exactly what the world might throw at you next. Thinking that, for all his faults, his father had never been a victim. Never. Seemed smarter all the time, the old man.

So, the lake was frozen over. Solid. Guy owned the station was ice fishing. Druggist said the locals hadn't seen it this cold, this long, in fifty years. Colter could picture the frozen lake just looking at the icebound creek. The waves along the isolated south shore, just a couple miles on ahead where the gravel road used to come down to a cement boat ramp, would be frozen up solid into little ice peaks from that sweep of north wind. He could imagine that deserted shoreline, could see the narrow inlet frozen hard and deep between the hills where the creek came down out of the red dirt pasture country. One time, back when he was a kid and the lake froze over, they had gone out to the inlet to skate in their street shoes and skip stones across the ice, and he had seen mallards and the drab little mud hens swimming around and around a few yards out from shore. He could imagine them swimming through the frozen night, keeping their little circle of water clear of ice.

Now, thinking again of the frozen lake, the straggler ducks and geese caught in this late spring storm, he could see them churning the water with their endless swimming and honking and quacking through the dark, long night of ice. He thought of the nightwatchman's little black truck, set to slow idle in Low or Drive 1, and how the truck might just crawl out onto the shoreline ice toward the circle of open water. He knew the water would be deep, just out from the steep little canyon walls. Just deep enough, he thought. So much for the truck. But even if it were found, they would never look for the nightwatchman's body under a sack of lime in the pit beneath old Myrtle's two-holer. Have to tip it back just to push the bastard in. Shoot, be just like Halloween again. All Saints' Eve at Easter. Have to kill him in the truck, though, or it'd be like trying to load up a dead horse by hand. The plan was getting a little complicated, but it was something to think about instead of his frozen feet. Hunt instead of hide. Colter liked that.

He walked ahead, breaking a path for Oliver wherever he could, dragging his feet a little, breaking down the deep blue snow of the shadowed creek bed into a path. The branches overhead still looked orange with the early, slanting sunlight. He paused at the edge of a drift to listen and Oliver nearly ran him over with his stumbling gait. He knew he had to do something quickly before the combination of cold and blood loss dropped Oliver in his own tracks. With both of them shot, doing anything but slow walking was going to be next to impossible.

The little creek with the made-up Indian name meandered in a loose diagonal across the home section and on through a series of loops and oxbows toward the northwest and the old river channel, lost now in the filling of the lake behind the Army Corp of Engineers' dam. The Tyree homestead was the only stretch of cleared ground along the creek for several miles. Another mile west and there were wooded pastures on either side, with plenty of cover and access to the network of dirt roads in case someone should come along. Beyond the bridge lay another wide pasture, at least a quarter section, where an escape corridor of woods ran from the creek all the way up behind Myrtle's old house in town. Right now the issue was the bridge, and they had at least a couple hundred yards yet to go.

If we could just stay out here and stay warm and not bleed to death, he thought. Then everything would work itself out. Time heals all, he thought again. That asshole has got to die first, he thought. It's the natural order of things. Colter clung to the idea through another hundred yards of snowbound struggle before his mind came back to the bridge.

He made Oliver rest for a moment against a fallen cottonwood log that spanned the creek while he thought about it some more. The tree's shallow pan of roots and soil, upended like a plate, gave Colter a chance to gain a little altitude above the surrounding willow thicket, but there was nothing to see except the silent woods along the creek. In the distance a crow called and another answered, but they were the wrong direction for the scattered grain. Ahead maybe another hundred yards or so, well within effective rifle range, lay the old WPA bridge, a graceful arch above the channel of the creek. It looked like one of those old Roman bridges made of stone, its concrete face pockmarked with swallow nests of mud on the upstream side, just as he remembered. The arch above and the gentle, rounded "U" of the streambed below made a shaded cave. The cover of woods ran ahead for maybe seventy-five feet, but the last few yards of creek bank had been bladed clear of trees and brush, the banks artificially sloped and rocked to prevent storm runoff from undermining the bridge abutments. Perfect field of fire.

"If we could get to the bridge," Colter whispered. "Not even past it. Just to it, we're home free."

"Wow," Oliver said. "Fucking brilliant. He's got to come down one side or the other. If he leaves the bridge, we've got a free pass to

Myrtle's house and town. He doesn't know anything about our intense firepower. Pop him whichever side he comes down. While he's deciding, somebody might even come along."

"I can see a little dry grass, some tumbleweed up under the edge on the left there," Colter said. "Might even get a signal fire going."

"Sure could use one of those about now," Oliver said. His voice was growing steadily weaker.

Then they heard the truck.

Chapter Thirty-one

Oliver was standing like a wounded horse, his bad side drooping a little, his head tilted slightly as if he was calling on all his strength just to stay upright. He had a lot of blood sloshing around inside, Colter knew, and if they didn't get past the bridge and get some help soon he was never going to make it.

Out of the wind, in the shelter of the deep creek channel now, the sun felt almost warm. Colter could feel it on his face, his forehead. They tried to stay on the west side of the meandering stream, where the sunlight came in low over the east bank and warmed them, and Colter began to dread the cold in the shadow of the bridge.

For a moment they listened as the pickup swung out onto the county road from the old home place, the engine noise distinct across the still, cold fields as the driver accelerated, and the thought occurred to Colter that maybe the bastard would just go away. Just drive on back to town, pack up his little rented room, and disappear. Maybe thinking he'd already killed them, have a day or so head start before anybody found their bodies. Made no sense though. Oliver was right. He would have heard them, Colter anyway, crashing away through the brush. Would have heard their pain. He would have to know the authorities would hunt him down for something like this. That he couldn't expect to escape the web with two men wounded, maybe one dead, one left to talk. No, Colter knew in his heart of hearts that he'd be back. They listened as the Toyota made full speed for the bridge.

"He has to know," said Oliver. "Just because he's a dumb ass don't mean he's stupid. Man's gotta know he drew blood."

"He knows. I'm just waiting for the sound of the truck door to open at the bridge." The wooded band of flat bottomland was only about fifty yards wide as it snaked its way between the two sloping hillsides of wheat toward the bridge.

The footing was treacherous, the going slow at best, but they were nearing the bridge now. Colter could see it clearly through the trees. Another twenty yards of cover and they would have to make a run for it. Colter listened for the sound of the pickup, but around them lay the silence of the frozen fields, the distant calling of crows. Not a breath of wind stirred on one of the most beautiful winter mornings Colter could remember.

"Great day to die, huh Cole?" Oliver said. It was as if he had read Colter's mind.

Then a slight rattle of metal, and Colter realized that the night-watchman was coasting down the long hill from the left, toward the bridge, with his engine off.

"It almost worked," Colter said. "Listen."

Oliver stopped dead in his tracks, cocked his head sideways like a spaniel, and listened, the grimace of pain on his face loosening for a moment while he relaxed and tried to concentrate.

"Now, Ollie. We got to go now, right now, or we don't make the bridge."

"Now," said Oliver.

Chapter Thirty-two

They struggled then through the last of the tangled bottom, stumbling, slipping, until without warning, the way those things always happen, Oliver tripped on a willow root washed out by the creek and hidden in a snowdrift. It caught his foot squarely at the ankle and held firm, while the rest of him sailed down a tight arc into the thin creek ice.

"Oh Jesus," Colter said, wedging the rifle in one motion under his bad arm and reaching for the back of Oliver's jacket collar. He snatched him up and out of the water, but not before Oliver was soaking head to foot in freezing water.

"Move," Colter whispered hoarsely. "It's now or never, Ollie, I don't give a fuck how wet you are or how much it hurts, go now."

"I really can't just now," Oliver said. "I really can't," but he stumbled onto his good foot and they took off, no caution now about keeping dry. They took to the stream bottom then, crashing through the thin ice, splashing like two spooked heifers, off balance with Oliver's bad ankle and Colter's shot arm tight against his side, but stumbling ahead, good arms flaying out for balance, sunlight hitting the flying spray and the dry snow blowing about in their wake.

"Got to get out now," said Oliver, pulling away. "Deep. Gonna get deep here, where they graded. Got to get out now," and he began scrambling madly up to the left, the clanking noise louder now, like the sound of a loose fender rattling across the iron cold, frozen ruts, the springs squeaking, the sounds ominous without the accompanying revving of the engine, as if they were being run to ground by a ghost truck. Oliver crawled toward the top with Colter pushing from behind, but then Colter lost his footing and slid back down into the icy water, the safe shadow of the bridge only a few yards ahead.

Colter knew they had to be quieter now, quickly, or lose their advantage. He managed to slow his mad rush into a careful stride at an angle up the bank to the bridge embankment, but he knew instantly that the tracks leading into this side and no tracks coming out the other would tell the tale.

The squeak of brakes then, while the nightwatchman, still unaware they had made it to the bridge, was quietly slowing the truck, opening the door now and clicking it silently shut.

They ducked under the concrete arch just as the nightwatchman's first footfall crunched into the snow on the roadbed above. The section mile line ran true east-west and crossed above a north-south loop in the creek's meandering path toward the northeast. Coming from the left, the nightwatchman had taken his huge bulk into the path of least resistance, no doubt a lifelong habit. He had stepped quietly out of his truck and was now checking the north side for tracks. Colter could see the man's shadow as a long, distorted shape emerging from the clean line of the guardrail shadow on the north side. He watched Oliver shaking uncontrollably with the cold. In the sunlight they might have survived hours as the day warmed, but here in the cold shade of the bridge, both soaking wet and weak from shock and loss of blood, Colter knew Oliver wouldn't last another fifteen minutes.

He could hear the man's footsteps in the snow, could hear when he stubbed his boot against the raised concrete curb, cursing quietly as he nearly fell then recovered his silence almost in midbreath, and Colter knew he had already scanned the creek bank looking for tracks and had found none on the downstream side. Colter had waited, immobile, trying to weigh his options, but Oliver, by now resting in the bare dirt up near the bridge abutment, was pointing weakly back upstream, where the nightwatchman would look next. Where he would clearly see their stumbling tracks.

Had he come to the upstream side first, Colter suddenly realized, all might have been lost. But he hadn't, and now he had to turn his back, if only for an instant, to cross the bridge. Colter knew in a heartbeat it was their one and only chance. There wouldn't be any others unless somebody decided, on this lovely Easter morning, to take a drive in the country.

Colter motioned for Oliver to be quiet, but he could see no warning was needed. Oliver was lying on his side again, looking out at nothing at all. Then, like a gathering storm, the crows came. Screaming, calling, Colter could hear them coming up from the southwest along the creek, looking for corn. Without another thought Colter climbed around and over Oliver along the dry dirt beneath the bridge toward the north side, watching the nightwatchman's shadow. When the shadow began to disappear, he climbed an extra step to peer over the concrete wall that served as a rail. Sure enough, the nightwatchman was slowly lumbering his bulk across the bridge. Undistracted by the crows, he already had a lever-action .30–30 at his shoulder, ready for whatever he might see on the upstream side.

Colter's blood was pounding in his ears and making his arm throb, but the pain had leveled off into a dull ache. Nothing he couldn't work through, thinking again of Leon, of the woman on the bathroom floor. *evil* Wondering how many others. He raised the little .22 silently, pulling the wire stock in against his shoulder and resting the barrel in the soft snow atop the bridge rail, nestling it down into the snow so that the short barrel would not move. He trained it on the massive head, thinking back to his endless, mind-numbing combat training and seeing the little barrel quite properly now as an extension of his index finger. Knowing that his life was about to change forever, he prayed quickly for Grace to be with him now and on the journey that lay ahead. Please don't move, Colter meant to say out loud, but not quite getting to it before the nightwatchman heard the tap of the tube barrel against the bridge rail and began a slow-motion turn to the right. Another little miracle, Colter thought. If the man had turned to his left, the direction the carbine was already leading . . . as it was the nightwatchman tried instead to pivot around to his right, leveling the rifle out as he came, but the turn was too far for those giant thighs, and it took a second too long to do it. There wasn't even time to think while Colter squeezed the trigger with a loud *pop* and the round went off and the nightwatchman seemed to pause late in his turn. He focused for a moment on Colter and the little gun, the muzzle of the carbine waving in slow circles in Colter's direction as he managed to shuffle his feet around to the right, and then Colter noticed the tiny spot, like a third eye, almost dead center of the man's right temple. The nightwatchman stood there for a moment as if he were merely lost in thought and trying desperately to comprehend the significance of what had just happened.

It didn't even go in, Colter thought.

The nightwatchman stood stock-still, his massive legs too close together from the turn, his huge weight poised delicately as an egg on end and his eyes locked on Colter's until he seemed to simply collapse where he stood, all his weight pushing straight down onto his buckling knees and it was over, the carbine falling harmlessly onto the snowy bridge, the little *pop* of the .22 absorbed like the snapping of a twig into the mottled dome of sunshine and blue sky and raucous, screaming crows.

Chapter Thirty-three

Colter kicked the carbine out of the nightwatchman's reach just in case, then checked him for a pulse. When he was sure, he climbed back down to Oliver, who was about to slide down off the narrow ledge of dirt bank next to the concrete and now lay half in, half out of the shelter of the bridge. His eyes were open, his left arm moving aimlessly as if he were trying to find someplace firm to put it, but he looked pretty bad.

"Okay, Bud, we got it made now. Let's get you some help."

"Told you that round was good," Oliver whispered while he tried to focus. "Won't be needing it now anyway, but you better let me have the gun back."

"I don't think I can carry you up the bank by myself, but if we can hook your arm over my shoulder . . ."

"I don't need any more help, Cole," he said, his stare suddenly focused, intent. His voice firmer. "Not now. But you're going to. Put the gun in my hand. I owe you that."

Colter looked at him. "You don't owe me anything. Hadn't been for you, I'd probably be laying down alongside Johnny about now."

"No. For what I brought down on your dad. Your whole family, shit. Hand me the gun. I owe you that," he said again, then tried to cough through clenched teeth.

"My dad?"

"Come on, man. You really didn't think your dad had anything to do with what happened in that jail cell did you?"

Oliver looked at him.

"Come on, man. Surely *you* didn't think that of him?"

"Jesus."

"Sonofabitch beat on me one too many times, Cole. Just once too often. Locked up drunk, slumped down against the bars with the door open onto the alley like that. Took less than a minute. Your dad did me a favor all right, but he couldn't have known. After Johnny, that sorry fucking white trash was a piece of cake. Shoot, after Johnny, they all were. Until the very last of it anyway."

All Colter could do was look at him, the man wasted, lying on his side and trying to talk through clenched teeth.

"Inside, man. It's all sloshy inside. You think I don't know what's happening here? Just place the gun in my hand. Don't think about it, white man. Like that shoe ad says, just do it. I handle this, you handle the rest. This shit's long overdue."

"What about Gladys? Can you get your lousy ass up for Gladys?"

"Joint tenancy, right of survivorship," he whispered. "No problem."

"The fuck you talking about?" Colter said, thinking suddenly, selfishly, of Marilyn, of his house, his other life. His only other life.

"The diner goes to her," Oliver whispered again, "along with the Airstream and even the goddamn teepee. I took care of it," he sighed *but he has lived that morning over and over again in his head, each time changing some minute detail, some nuance of movement or stance, and always to no good end, until at last the pain of it all is like an old and trusted friend, without whom he cannot imagine living.*

He has played the memory out a million, million times, as if his head were a stupid Walkman with the stop/eject button broken and the only way to make it stop would be to smash the thing to pieces. Now, going on into yet another day with the thing smashed after all, their voices, the scuffling noises their shoes made in the cinders between the crossties, even the squeak of the wire and the final popping sound of the little .22, fade slowly away into the hot, empty distance. The image of that distant time diminishes, shrinking toward infinity as if trapped between the rails until the sight, the sound, the very memory of the two of them together begins to evaporate into a white-hot, shimmering mirage of sunflowers and September noon . . .

memory of brother's death

❧ Tuesday, April 5, 1994

Chapter Thirty-four

Alone with his thoughts while he waited at the bridge, Colter had weighed his options very carefully, and in the end he knew he had done what he had to do.

The rest of Sunday and all day Monday had been a blur of cursory medical attention, some detailed probing by both county law enforcement officials and Oklahoma Highway Patrol investigators, and finally a third night in the bridal suite, with Colter's rig temporarily impounded in place as evidence. He had sweat out the crime scene photographer taking shots of footprints in the melting snow, holding his breath they wouldn't backtrack and discover the old cellar, but with their focus instead on unraveling the actual sequence of events at the bridge, they considered the dog a minor footnote.

The hole in his shoulder turned out to be really only a flesh wound, with one tiny chip dislodged where the round just nicked the bone of his upper arm, but in the end the company decided to place him on medical leave anyway, his Class 8 license temporarily suspended due to injuries. The local authorities agreed to look the other way while he used his tractor as personal transportation only, without pulling a load. Now, with the sky completely clear in the west, the reefer van finally roadworthy and awaiting a replacement driver and Colter's tractor idling at the four-way stop, he knew there would have been consequences, serious entanglements, if he hadn't acted quickly.

Decisively. That was the word. Colter reached behind the seat for the Stetson he hadn't worn in three days. He slapped the brim, positioned it just so, then checked out the new Cowboy Colter in his side mirror. Seemed like he hadn't been able to act decisively in years. Saving it all up for now, when it counted. First thing had been to retrieve his little .32 from the Toyota glove box and toss it far away from the bridge, without any telltale tracks, where he could pick it up later on his way out of town. Second was to wipe the tube gun and shell casing clean of his own bloody prints and place the gun carefully back in Oliver's right hand.

With both details out of the way, nobody seemed to seriously question Colter's version of events when he called for help on the night-watchman's CB. By sheer coincidence Colter had been delayed in Fairview, his hometown, over the Easter weekend for emergency road repairs. After a frustrating day and night, he had driven out early to look over the family farm, his inheritance, actually, when he ran into Oliver Lonewolf, an old childhood friend, hunting rabbits with a little .22 caliber toy rifle. The way he told it, the nightwatchman, probably sleep deprived from his nighttime rounds and up early for a stand in the old barn, had accidentally fired twice in their direction, mistaking Colter's dog for a coyote and nailing him with the second shot. When they tried to warn the officer off, a third round coming straight into the chest-high Johnson grass at Oliver's headgear had dropped them both. As well as they could, they made a run for it, convinced after the third shot the nightwatchman would rather kill them and call it a hunting accident than risk trying to talk his way out of it. Sure enough, the rampaging officer had cut off their escape with an attempted ambush from the bridge.

He told how Oliver, with an incredibly lucky shot even considering his service record, had used his last round to drop the nightwatchman, rifle in hand, right beside his truck. Clearly Oliver had saved Colter's life, only to later die from internal bleeding and exposure before Colter could get medical help. In support of his story the drugstore owner and town councilman had later proven a welcome ally. The clincher was a belated background check of the nightwatchman's own violent record from a string of small midwestern towns over the last dozen years, which turned up another and now highly questionable "hunting accident."

Colter didn't figure there was much point in mentioning the trouble at the bar the night before. Just complicate matters, and he was pretty sure no one there at the time would volunteer any information, either eager to avoid a real inquiry or just grateful to be rid of the bastard. Certainly no point in bringing up Oliver's old man forty years later, either. Lot of fucking good that would do. With the newspaperman gone years ago, along with most of the town, there was nobody left to care.

Gladys was devastated but resigned. Tough as nails. Suggesting that whatever horrors Oliver might have committed in the past, and she knew about a few of them all right, the bill was paid in full. He'd been good to Myrtle, too, for all these years. Blood was always thicker with Indians, she said. The tribal services and BIA people would step in now, with Oliver gone, to handle old Myrtle, move her in with some distant relations until the end. During Colter's last, brief visit, one silent moment between them as he cupped Myrtle's frail hands in his was enough to let her know that both Oliver and Johnny had finally found their star path. Now she could carry the peace of that knowledge to her grave. And sure enough, Gladys would get to keep the diner. Oliver really had seen to it. Probably couldn't stay camped out indefinitely on tribal land, but she could move the little Airstream out back of the diner if she wanted. She'd be okay. Or hit the road, like her daddy. "What the hell, the thing has wheels," she'd said.

Rae Lynn was an unfinished story. Colter's halfhearted curiosity had gone nowhere. Just as well, he thought. No reason to complicate his life even more. Probably wouldn't have recognized her anyway. In the quiet, hidden corner of his heart reserved just for her, she would be forever fourteen, her auburn hair in a sexy little flip, and for some reason usually wearing a fuzzy, pale green boatneck sweater and a rust-brown, short pleated skirt. He would content himself with visiting her in dreams.

Late in the afternoon, after retrieving the pistol and posting a hastily drawn quitclaim deed to the farm in lieu of an appearance bond in case they wanted him for a coroner's hearing, Colter plastered the gates with red and white No Hunting and No Trespassing signs. Backtracking alone into the snowy bottom to bury old Leon, he found much of the snow gone but the ground still frozen, his task impossible.

The solution was as obvious as it was appropriate. It was easy enough, even with his left arm in a sling, to drag Leon onto the cellar floor beside the wooden table and then pry out part of the keystone row of rotten brick from atop the cellar dome with a tire iron from the truck. The hard part had been not to fall in with the collapsing hillside. What the hell, it was his place anyway. Since he couldn't risk selling it now, he guessed he could do whatever else he wanted with it. No debt on the place, so he wouldn't have to renew the lease. Might even come back someday, park a trailer up the hill where the old house used to be, and take up Oliver's vigil. Never had been anything but a footpath up to the house, no real road access, so there wouldn't likely be anyone sneaking in to carry off the antique brick. Gourd vines and devil's-claw would cover the depression by summer's end. Not a proper burial, but at least a final resting place. Somehow seemed more permanent to Colter than a shaky tabletop. What's a proper burial anyway, but a little dirt in your face, he thought. Honor the dead by keeping their secrets. Dust to dust, amen. A long and prosperous life was the thing. And there was no way Colter, or anyone else, could give that back to Johnny now. Or Oliver. Christ, at his age there wasn't even enough time left to give himself one.

Turned out some things were, after all, irreversible.

Chapter Thirty-five

The telephone booth in front of the diner was a good deal more comfortable this time around. He fished a couple of quarters from his pocket and laid them on the cold chrome shelf beneath the phone box, then took one and dropped it in the slot. Late-afternoon sunlight coming through the glass gave the booth a cozy feel, even with the door propped open, and it took only a moment to anonymously set authorities on the trail of another body, this one by now probably just a thin scatter of bones along the riverbank south of town.

With his voice disguised in that handy *peón* accent, he became a Mexican farm worker passing through on his way north, fishing for *gatos* along the river. In halting English he tried to tell them where to search.

"Es that sandy place where to fish below you Indian dances," he said, and then he hung up; another long-overdue debt paid down now, his guardian angel could maybe take a break.

Pretty sure it would be enough, too. Couldn't hurt to keep the law busy looking in the other direction. One hidden body at a time, he thought. Enough to keep the dreams coming. Any better weather and he would have paid his respects in person, hoping after this long that whoever she was, her soul, if such a thing existed, would have finally found some peace.

He paused at the frontage road stop sign, the engine vibrating with its rough, familiar idle right up through the floorboards into his bare feet. With both tanks topped off, about a million miles of open interstate waiting in one direction, Marilyn and home in the other, Colter still couldn't make up his mind.

He looked down at the blue plastic water dish where the water had sloshed a little onto the floor, felt the passenger seat strangely empty beside him. The cab was suddenly very lonely. Right enough, he was goddamn sure going to miss the mutt. He could feel his eyes tearing up with that tug again, the homeward pull of the westbound lane, those invisible bands stretching out across the High Plains from the first rank of mountains east of Albuquerque. For nearly thirty years New Mexico had been the Middle Kingdom, navel of his universe. But as he looked about at the shape and color of the countryside, the low evening sun slanting brightly off the green rolling fields of new spring wheat, he began to waver. With the window down Colter could smell spring coming, could smell damp earth behind the thaw.

He thought about his own blood, and the blood of his friend, and of his mortal enemy, and even his dog's blood for chrissake, spilled on the land. His own land now. In some primal way he had finally fought his way home, the blood from the battle still staining his own flesh, his hands. Removing the little pistol from the nightwatchman's paper sack on the dash and rolling the strangely cold metal of the barrel across his forehead, touching the muzzle to his temple, he thought of his father lying in that sunken, unmarked grave on the little cedar knoll above the river. Pictured the melting of the snow above him, the coming grass. Finally at peace, their differences reconciled after all, Colter felt the farm was truly his, felt it as surely as if he had finished chopping out the cedars, had worked the place all his life. He actually felt as if his father would want him to have it now. In the old man's good graces at last. Next time through on I-40 he'd take the time to see about a stone. Colter replaced the pistol in the paper sack and stowed it securely away in the glove box.

Reaching inside his jacket pocket and cupping his fingers around the warm vinyl of the little coffin-shaped medal box that held Oliver's Purple Heart, he felt a twinge of guilt. He'd been sorely tempted to leave the medal with Gladys, what with a full-dress military funeral in the planning stages. But just having the thing in his possession would have raised too many questions. Too bad, too. She could have pinned it on old Oliver as a burial offering, the perfect accessory to that moth-eaten coyote skin he was going down in. Wondering just exactly what the burial detail would think about that one if it turned out to be an open-casket funeral.

How many just like Oliver, he wondered, had he trained and sent on over to die during his three years, four months, and seventeen days on active duty? God, he was nothing but a scared kid himself then. Could have volunteered, but didn't. Waited instead, willing to go, for the call that never came. Feeling again through his bare feet the familiar, impatient idle of the diesel engine, he wondered how many *shame that don't fit* of those kids who had fought his war for him were out there right now, still trying to find their way home. Young boys whose lives really ended back in the sixties or seventies in some wet, stinking corner of a jungle he couldn't even clearly imagine, boys turned too soon into old men, the walking dead only now beginning to fall. From now on, whenever he could, he'd be an Angel of Grace himself, throwing a few extra wadded-up dollar bills out the window at the ragged souls hanging around the truck stop on-ramps.

Colter could feel a subtle difference in his chest. There seemed a tightening of the elastic bands from his end, as if a sort of equilibrium might be in the offing. A shift in his own personal center of gravity. A little time on his hands, enough money left in his stash to last until the next dispatch, Colter figured he might just make a run over D.C. way. Take along a little masking tape, pencil in the name, and stick Oliver's medal right onto that wall. What the fuck. "Drink a beer and shed a tear," just like the man said.

His decision made, he pushed his way smooth as oil through the first couple of gears and found himself crawling at slow idle beneath the underpass, banking out of habit toward the outside for a hard left up the ramp toward Okie City and points east.

tethers
of old life

He could feel, along with the quick whine and fall of the unencumbered engine that accompanied each shift up the grade, a breaking away, one by one, of the tethers that bound him to his old life. He had not called Marilyn back as he had promised, not that she'd believe much of it anyway, and dispatch had relayed no anxious message from her end. When he got around to calling in his own sweet time Marilyn might notice a certain lightening of the load; they would talk, maybe try to work things out without the added weight of anger. In the long run, she'd probably be better off without him. The kids had been lighter than air and unconnected for years. They would feel nothing. Maybe he'd see them at Christmas, maybe not.

No wiser than the Colter Wayne Tyree of five days ago, he still could not say what lay ahead. But he was definitely a changed man. That much was clear. War, even a little war, changed you. He had always suspected as much; now he knew it with certainty. That vague dread, like despair in future tense, was gone. He had been to the river, all right. Christ, he had been trapped in a cellar with a dead body, and that turned out to be the easy part. The nightwatchman had obviously killed before. Seeing Leon slide down a glass wall for the thousandth time, and watching poor, wilted Prairie Flower flopped upside down like a rag doll against those massive, bruising hips, Colter doubted he would ever feel any remorse. He could imagine looking over his shoulder for a week or so, until after the coroner's hearing, but it all felt pretty solid. So, he'd have to live with the nightmares for a while longer, his own private, hidden body syndrome, but aside from that and a little lingering claustrophobia, there was truly nothing he could imagine being afraid of ever again. Colter knew from the river and his first innocent encounter with evil that you couldn't always stop it. He knew now you just had to kill it when you could.

Gearing slowly up the ramp and away from the fierce western sunset flaring in his passenger-side mirror, Colter was filled once more with a keen, almost palpitating anticipation for dusk and the flowing river of lights. He could imagine Coyote, back to the west a few miles, slowly emerging from a melting snowdrift in a grimace of bared teeth and bone, smiling like an April Fool.

Immediately upon pulling out into the sparse late-afternoon stream of eastbound I-40 traffic, his gaze reaching out toward the far horizon, Colter felt a flutter in his chest, as if his rib cage held a butterfly. He was reminded of a wonderful line he'd read one time, what was that guy's name anyway, that clever Greek, when quite suddenly and for no apparent reason he could feel his heart beating in his breast like the heart of a young calf. Just beyond the sudden wall of pain he could sense the edge again, a fiery border drawing near, then nearer yet.

Unafraid now, he slipped across.